PRAISE F(

The Vortex Effect is intelligent, compelling, and fun. Laced with the keen observations of a first-rate physician, the irreverence of a life-long musician, and the musings of a serious wonk, *Vortex* takes aim at almost all of contemporary America's sacred cows, with humor, passion and suspense.

Elinor Burkett—*New York Times* best selling author

Dr. Wayne Liebhard has seen the best and the worst of American medicine, music and politics. And he'd like to see a few things changed! Thank goodness he's created Derek Mann to share his ideas with us. Equal parts drama, social commentary, and metaphysical exploration, Mann's story, at heart, is every person's search for happiness and meaning in a society that wants to paint us all the same shade of gray. This book is bound to stimulate conversations long after readers have put it down. Bravo!

Dr. Ann Korbel—editor

The Vortex Effect is a riveting adventure. It grabs your attention and sucks you into a remarkable twisting, turning suspense tale, while simultaneously forcing you to question the boundaries of your own existence. Wayne Liebhard's protagonist, Dr. Derek Mann, is the perfect conduit for the trip, and this ride will leave you permanently changed. I especially enjoyed the music theme that runs through the book. One gets the feeling that Dr. Mann would rather be on stage playing his guitar than in the ER.

Jim Donna of The Castaways—co-author of *Liar, Liar*.
Member Minnesota Rock & Country Hall of Fame.

If you find it hard to believe the doctor you've come to enjoy, and think you know, is much more than a white coat learning digital record keeping, then you must read *The Vortex Effect*. If you've worked every day with a doctor who has an extraordinary affection for his undergrad alma mater, and will do great rock 'n' roll after just two beers, then get ready for a real ER doc having a mind-altering experience in Wayne Liebhard's *The Vortex Effect*.

Dave Durenberger
U.S. Senator (R-MN) 1978-95
St. John's University '55

Dr. Wayne Liebhard's most recent novel, *The Vortex Effect*, is a fascinating combination of a strange internal experience combined with a unique mystery. Dr. Liebhard is a respected physician who shows great perception about what ails health care in 2015. This is a well written novel that rivets one's attention and is very hard to put down.

Thomas A. Stolee, M.D.—past president,
Minnesota Medical Association

PRAISE FOR *ELEPHANTS IN THE EXAM ROOM*

Elephants in The Exam Room is a powerful book. The author, Dr. Wayne Liebhard, picks apart the American health care system and shows why we are in a health care crisis and what needs to be done about it. What I found extraordinary about this book is that Liebhard not only candidly exposes the problems within America's health care system, but he also offers realistic and practical solutions. I hope every American reads this book and voices their concern, even outrage, at what's going on.

Karen Coiffi-Ventrice of BookPleasures.com

Health care is a very touchy and complicated subject, so let me refer you to what I think is the best treatise I have ever read on this subject: *Elephants in the Exam Room* by Dr. Wayne Liebhard.

Minnesota State Representative Michael Beard

While I was in the U.S. Senate trying to change the practice of medicine by changing the way Medicare finances patient care, Wayne and doctors like him were growing frustrated. First in their efforts to meet patient needs and demands, and then by the changes in the system, in the life styles of practitioners, and the growing emphasis by folks like me in changing practice behavior from the outside in. For those of us who believe that community and family health professionals, not bionic medicine men, are the key to improved access, quality, and cost, this nicely-written plea by a Minnesota doc and friend is a good read.

Former U.S. Senator Dave Durenberger,
director, National Institute of Health Policy

Elephants in The Exam Room is a warning to patients and a wake-up call to physicians. With a blunt tongue and a few pointed fingers, Dr. Liebhard debunks health care myths and demystifies the dangerous doublespeak of today's health care debate. Every reader should heed Dr. Liebhard's warning before there are only elephants left in the room, and no doctors to be found.

Twila Brase, RN, PHN, president,
Citizen's Council on Health Care

This book is a "must-read" for anyone interested in returning control of their health care decisions to consumers and their physicians, and away from government regulators and HMO executives.

Thomas A. Stolee, M.D., past president,
Minnesota Medical Association

WORKS BY WAYNE LIEBHARD

Fiction

The Vortex Effect

Nonfiction

Elephants In The Exam Room
(The Big Picture Solution To
Today's Health Care "Crisis")

Elephants In The Exam Room
(The Seven Things You Need To Know
About Today's Health Care "Crisis")

Music

Here—In Flyover Country (Original Album)

Music Videos

For The Solid Gold Band

THE VORTEX EFFECT

To Joe –
Long live
the VFW! John &
Delores! [illegible]

A NOVEL

WAYNE D. LIEBHARD, M.D.

NORTH LOOP BOOKS | MINNEAPOLIS, MN

North Loop Books
322 First Avenue N, 5th floor
Minneapolis, MN 55401
612.455.2294
www.NorthLoopBooks.com

Grateful acknowledgment is made toward those who have allowed the use of their actual names and/or businesses.

ISBN-13: 978-1-63413-488-0
LCCN: 2015917081

Cover Design by Alan Pranke
Typeset by B. Cook

Printed in the United States of America

Author's note:

The mechanics of writing a book may boil down to the individual efforts of an author, but the substance of the result is composed of many diverse ingredients, including some borrowed from the experiences and insights of others.

I am blessed to be able to tap into an incredible network of individuals who remain uninhibited in expressing their insights on the world and who remain equally open to subjecting those insights to critique. To them, I offer deep gratitude.

My deepest gratitude is reserved for Joy, Reilly, and Erinn, who most closely interacted with me during the process of simultaneously practicing medicine and writing another book. The support, and critique, from one's family are the most profound of influences. Beyond that, Joy again earns the credit for her unique ability to guide me through the big picture, and Reilly for his remarkable legal, editing, and philosophical expertise.

Special thanks also to the Effertz family, especially Kate for providing me her amazing inspirational painting ("The Vortex"), and her father, Dick, a man who is no stranger to the vortex . . .

Also, immense gratitude goes to my numerous pre-readers. Many, given a complex novel, took the time to provide feedback, spot inconsistencies, and help keep the vortex storyline on track. I cannot thank them enough.

In no particular order, they are: Lynn Lombardi; Linda Jacques; Dr. Ann Korbel; Mike McKinley; Erinn Liebhard; Dr. Rick Carlson; Eileen Effertz; Earl and Sonja Sherburne; Senator Dave Durenberger; Andy Halvorsen; Pat Fitzgerald; and Dr. Tom Stolee.

Thank you also to Reilly Liebhard and Thom Woodward for special editorial guidance, and to anyone else who may have provided assistance that I have forgotten to mention.

Parts of this book were written at various places in the great state of Minnesota, as I experienced its wonders along with fellow adventurers Scott Lombardi; Dick Effertz; Stan Effertz; Andy Halvorsen; Zach Effertz; Don Effertz; and Neil Sorenson.

While significant research has been done during the writing of this novel, any misrepresentations or errors therein are entirely the fault of the author.

"If you find a path with no obstacles,
it probably doesn't lead anywhere."

Frank A. Clark

Prologue

Most of us suspect—deep down—that at some point along our journey, we will experience a significant life-changing event. We know, because we've seen it happen countless times in the lives of others.

We may embrace or fear the thought, because we know that the event could be pleasant, or it could be disastrous. But—deep down—we all know it's out there. We just don't know when it will happen.

So we go on, living our lives—waiting it out and assuring ourselves that we are unique, or at least the time period in which we live is somehow unique. To some extent this is true, as no two lives have ever been completely the same. Despite the fact that history may have a fabled tendency to "repeat itself," it remains just that—history.

My significant life-changing event started out looking anything but unique. I never would have suspected that my experience would commence with merely sitting down and tipping my head back. And, of all the places in the world to be when my big event happened, I was sitting in a tree?

Seriously?

When it happened, though, there was no mistaking it. Life was never going to be close to being the same again for me, or—as I found out later—for most of the people I really cared about . . .

Chapter 1

Beep beep . . . beep beep . . . beep beep . . . beep . . .

My eyes popped wide open—into a red digital glare that proclaimed 3:16 a.m.

I reflexively did a blind one-handed sweep for the pager, just as the bedside phone began to jangle—until it got knocked off its cradle in a wild search for the beeping demon.

Bolting to a sitting position on the call room slab, I flipped on the light, palmed the pager with one hand, and put the phone to my ear with the other.

My semiconscious mind was presented with a simultaneous audiovisual greeting: Code Blue Room 412.

With the snooze-button reflex long since beaten out of me, my brain proceeded to direct my legs to run down the hallway—as the rest of me began waking up and realizing that I was fast approaching a train wreck.

As I hit room 412, my neurons had begun conversing, and the world went into hyperspeed and I yelled orders and we did CPR and oxygen and IV fluids and more CPR and IV meds and more orders and more meds and we grabbed the paddles and we charged the defibrillator and I put the paddles on his chest and pushed the button and . . . Hit the brakes!

"Dammit, man!" I muttered to myself, gripping the steering wheel. "Your wandering mind is no doubt going to kill you long before some irate ER patient decides to plug you with a .44."

Of course, I thought, *your wandering mind did snap back just in time to send a two-millisecond action potential through your spinal cord to your quadriceps and gastrocnemius muscles—enough to hit the brakes before the eight-point buck running across the road became your traveling companion in the front seat.*

A long sigh passed through my lips. Shame what it would have done to the vintage Mustang fastback as well. Taking it out on a trip like this was something I'd never done before, and after this would probably never do again. Original 1965 repair parts just weren't growing on trees anymore.

It had seemed like a great idea at its inception: take the old Stang out for the trip up north to start my vacation. I have always conspired to combine my pleasures within what seems to be my most limited resource—time. Of course, we all pick our own poison. I'd absorbed enough med school psychology and seen enough of *Dr. Phil* to know that just about everything any of us does has some underlying purpose.

As to that, my curiosity continues regarding what exactly drives me to my distractions—though I think I'm beginning to get a handle on it, and that's largely what this vacation, and this trip, was about. Fortunately, I don't have anything to hold me back from taking off whenever I want, except an ER contract signed "Derek Mann, MD," which requires me to work a certain number of weeks each year. After a few years of practicing medicine, I was finally learning the value of, at times, completely separating myself from it.

So, I'm driving down this road toward northern Minnesota in a 1965 Mustang fastback—deep in thought as usual, and oblivious to the world—not entirely unusual. Absolutely clueless as to how my life would dramatically change over the next few days . . .

Earlier, I had hit the road to begin my trip. Being a guy who believes that original should really mean original, the Stang remained equipped with its factory radio—fortunately in this case a rare slide bar AM/FM. My choices for listening would get more restricted as I passed further north, but for now, all of the Twin Cities stations came in nicely. The "Morning Crew" on KQRS 92.5 FM was finishing up taking "equal shots at everyone," with Tom Barnard leading the charge. As I travelled even further, I probably still would get to hear the beginning of *Garage Logic* before AM 1500 faded out, where there was a good chance that Joe Soucheray would remind me that I didn't have the right not to be offended.

Knowing this was going to be a several-hour trip, I decided to risk the diuretic effect on my kidneys and stop for a coffee. Pulling off at the next exit, I turned and rolled into a gas station parking lot. Once inside the dimly lit structure, I found an old coffeepot with enough limescale layers to tempt a geologist. From behind the counter, a face with about three days of stubble announced: "You know, man, getting your coffee here is like buying muffins at the hardware store."

I laughed. "Think I'll just get a Coke."

Back in the car, I passed the turnoff to my hometown and stole a glance at the old burg while driving by. Small towns, especially *hometown* small towns, generate quite a range of emotion in people. Some growing up there are so enamored that they plant fifty-foot-deep roots, and others quickly kick the provincial dust off their boots and ignore the rearview mirror. I'm the type that kicked off the dust, but still takes the occasional glance in the mirror.

Don't let anyone who grew up in or near a small town try to blow smoke up your ass and tell you that they got out of Dodge unchanged—for good or for bad. If it were possible to completely ignore the psychological imprinting of a small town, hundreds of country singers would be washing dishes instead of cutting records.

As with many small towns in this state or any state, what catches your eye first is the structure that towers above the one-, two-, and three-story buildings that make up the town. This, of course, would be the town water tower. Just one quick glimpse at this one always gets my neuronal synapses sizzling in recall.

It's darker than hell, windy, and I am standing on top of the *ball* of that damn thing. Holding the label of "smart kid" of my high school class, there was no doubt in my mind that on this night—or most nights—the residents of this burg who gave a shit about any such stuff were convinced that I was home with a book stuffed up against my nose.

True enough, a book was stuffed there on occasion. On many more occasions, I was out trying to test the laws of physics (while risking self-inflicted death) in various pursuits, including attempting the replication of the water tower stunt in every other town in our high school conference. Stunts like that, my general aversion to hypocrisy, and the fact that I personally am far from perfect, always serve to remind me to be careful when considering passing judgment. Societal trend is, of course, much more disturbing than any individual case—and in my individual case (so I rationalize), at least I stopped that crazy crap after adolescence.

Another synaptic sizzle, and I'm standing beneath that same albatross as a Greyhound bus pulls up and stops with an ear-biting screech of brakes and an olfactory assault of diesel fumes. A few of us are standing there awaiting the arrival of our new foreign exchange student. Curiosity, most likely, as our parochial eyes had never laid sight on anyone from Australia, or been treated to those wonderful figures of speech couched in that delicious accent.

The poor girl had flown a long way just to get to Minnesota, and then was herded onto the Greyhound and driven across the prairie for this auspicious arrival. By this time she was obviously quite fatigued, and she emerged from the bus wiping her brow and making our acquaintance by announcing: "I'm all knocked up!"

Wow, I thought—*a new record. Usually you have to spend at least two or three days in this town to end up in that condition . . .*

Humor aside, back in the day that *condition* ended up afflicting more of us than it should have. The only morning sickness any of us should have had to deal with was the leftover effects of the previous night's revelry.

There were, of course, alternatives to help avoid becoming afflicted with the condition. These, of course, would require more forethought than my older brother's oft-mentioned jocular reference—where he was likely referring to something other than railroad punctuality when he noted: "The Great Northern always pulls out on time."

To that end, doctors had advised their patients for many years previous that a safe and effective form of birth control was an intrauterine device containing copper that was inserted through the cervix and left in place for an entire decade. Parents had advised their children for many years previous that a safe and effective form of birth control was an extrauterine device containing copper (and Abe Lincoln's face) that was inserted between the knees and held in place for an entire date.

Around the corner, Main Street ran through the middle of town. Numerous intersecting side streets contained the usual cornucopia of small-town homes, full of people living out an existence that I never failed to think about every time I drove by them—an existence represented in archetypal multiplicity across a vast nation—a sobering, yet somehow soothing, existence.

Main Street had a handful of businesses, and of course, its parade of bars. Rumor had it that several years back, the

Chamber of Commerce was putting together a pamphlet and ended up scrapping the idea of including any pictures of downtown, because they couldn't take one at any angle that didn't have a bar in it.

At the ripe old age of thirteen, I was playing in one of those bars in a rock band. It was an incredible experience for a thirteen-year-old. I saw things I wasn't ready to see, but made no great effort to close my eyes. It all went well until they eventually relieved us of our "contract" because we kept filling the place with teenagers.

By then I'd passed the old burg and was winging my way through the countryside. About two miles out of town, I passed the sign for Saint James Church. *The synapses are really getting a workout today,* I thought. My mind spun back again, and I saw myself dressed in a black and white cassock—a twelve-year-old altar boy listening to Father Bernard Dean giving one of his incredible sermons. It wasn't one of those where it seemed like we Catholics were inevitably doomed to hell no matter what we did—I had already learned to ignore those. This was one with a subject that he repeated often enough to let us know how important he thought it was, but not so often as to make us tune it out.

The man was obviously very learned, and obviously had made a few trips around the block—and, I suspect, around the world. He often spoke with great clarity and veracity about the subject of history. One of his favorite points to make was a comparison between the fall of the

Roman Empire and our current society's behavior as an attempt to replicate it. To me he was clear and convincing and spot on, and I was fascinated to be sitting in a little country church listening to him. Not detracting from his mystique were several rumors about his past, some partially substantiated, that in various ways lent an explanation as to why he ended up in our little neck of the woods, and why he behaved the way he did.

He had worked for the CIA . . . he had been a top national labor negotiator . . . he had been previously engaged to be married before a breakup that made him choose the priesthood . . . he was currently in the witness protection program . . .

No matter what, he was a tough taskmaster and an engaging speaker. Fighting his own demons, he was also a self-proclaimed alcoholic. Our suspicions had been aroused long before the Sunday when he arrived for Mass three sheets to the wind and announced the fact to us from the pulpit.

There are some things that twelve-year-old altar boys aren't likely to forget—like going to the rectory to find your priest who hasn't shown up for Mass and discovering him sitting in a chair in his underwear on the back porch, cigarette in mouth, gin bottle in one hand, revolver in the other—shooting at gophers.

The highway whined beneath me as four narrow fourteen-inch tires ate up the pavement—new red-line replicas I had installed the week before.

The scenery had slowly changed from dense northern city suburbs to thinner, older housing developments to scattered houses and smaller towns punctuating the landscape. Stands of thick pine, bare halfway up their trunks, began dominating the vegetation.

I had exited 94 West and gone through the town of Clearwater to get to County Road 8, which would take me to Saint Cloud, from which I would head directly northward.

County Road 8 between the Twin Cities and Saint Cloud is a two-lane road full of commuters, vacationers, truck drivers, and guys like me—headed on a trip "up north."

Guys pulling boats, campers, and trailers made up most of the traffic on my side of the road. The other side, headed back toward Minneapolis, was mostly cars and a few semitrailer trucks hauling a variety of cargo. One of those eighteen-wheelers was making its way toward me on the opposite side of the road when it happened.

I was deep in my own thoughts when I was rapidly shaken out of my stupor—by a loud bang coming from the driver's front side of the Stang. The car took a sudden and violent swing to the left, which took me completely off guard. As I crossed the center line and fought to turn the steering wheel right—against the pull of the left front tire blowout—the impending impact with an oncoming Mack eighteen-wheeler suddenly became obvious.

What flashed through my mind were not the details of my life, but instead the words "Am I really going to die on the *first* day of my vacation?"

Chapter 2

I wouldn't have been driving on this road in the first place, had it not been the weekend of Minnesota's fishing opener. The weekend was a perfect excuse to embark on a trip to try to deal with the numerous thoughts that had been distracting me. Too many questions about life, and a few leftover ones about medicine, were plaguing the hell out of me.

I didn't always know I wanted to become a doctor, and I still don't primarily think of myself as one. So, I didn't lie to the admissions committee and tell them I'd known since age two that I'd like to spend the rest of my life probing people's orifices while wearing rubber gloves.

I've always had a lot of interests, and an equal amount of difficulty deciding how much time to apply to any or all of them. So, I waffled—and attempted to dabble in all of them: Jack of all trades, master of maybe a couple. As a result, I've had an incredible amount of interesting experiences in life—though I'm still left wondering how I ever made the *big* decisions. Even though I really don't believe in this stuff, I still can't seem to shake the idea of questioning how much of my life happens as a result of conscious decision, and how much may be in some way predestined, or somehow guided.

A trip to a Chinese restaurant, however, is all it takes to prove to me that some decisions are uniquely mine. Hand me a menu, and I'm in deep shit. It'll take me an hour to make a decision. Fortunately, put a patient ahead of me with a complex medical problem, and I get right to it. If I absolutely had to vacillate about something, my proclivity would be toward the former rather than the latter. Somewhere along the line, it also became plainly obvious that I could be a doctor and a musician, but not so easily a musician and a doctor.

What I never did become was a very good driver, probably because I'm so damn impatient. Because of that, I use the time that a long driving trip affords me to help organize the numerous thoughts going through my head into some cohesive worldview that I can manage to live with. That also detracts from my driving skills, but I do it anyway—and on this trip, I'd be doing a lot of thinking. Sometimes I wish I could just stop asking myself so damn many questions. But questioning, unfortunately, and fortunately, is the essence of the human condition.

Part of my cohesive worldview is dealing with my own demons, faults, and insecurities. Part of it is dealing with attempting to discern where the hell I fit in a world that seems to have lost its bearings when it comes to any sense of boundaries and subsequent individual responsibility.

I love to take care of patients and be part of their lives, but every day I see what some people do to themselves. People should have the right to choose to live sixty Keith Richards years instead of eighty Margaret Thatcher years, but I keep wondering if they should have the right to expect society (and therefore me) to pay for their wild ride through life.

"What do you mean, I can't have an MRI?" a patient had demanded of me two days earlier. He had twisted his knee after attempting some sort of backward jump on his skateboard that same day.

"I didn't say you couldn't have an MRI," I had replied. "I said that, based on your exam, it's too early to get one at this point." On that particular day, my expertise was less than appreciated.

As a physician, I regularly get to see people at their best, and at their worst. The practice of medicine can be an arduous task, but it ends up being an interesting window on the issues of the world, and it is almost impossible to ignore the view, or to avoid making comparisons between the two, when trying to make sense of either one.

It's likely that I'm way too much of a hard-ass when it comes to what I expect from other people—yet again, I expect even more from myself. I am fiercely loyal, independent, and thorough— and along the way I am also capable of perturbation, procrastination, and mental masturbation. The road to sanity, largely, is coming to grips with the things you don't like about yourself, and that's a road I'm still traveling on. Fortunately, those who know me well enough understand me, but there are others that I frustrate the hell out of.

So I go on from day to day, trying to make sense of it all, secretly hoping, and expecting, that something decisive will happen that brings it all into focus. Perhaps that explains my crazy vestigial recall, going back further than I can remember, where one day some sort of scientific discovery (probably in physics) will happen that will literally rock the world—and it will be something that has been right under our noses all along. No doubt this is why I would like nothing more than to be driving on a gravel road in the country late one night and stumble across an honest-to-God alien craft—one that looks nothing like a fuzzy picture of one of Grandma's pie tins tossed into the air.

It would be fantastic, but I just don't think it's going to happen. I'm probably jaded because by now we were all supposed to be zipping around in flying cars, and I don't see them arriving anytime soon. Of course, we did get smartphones, and no one really saw them coming either. Ultimately, the one thing that keeps me going is the realization that, through my actions, I have lived a life with no regrets—except one: a beautiful face that has continued to haunt me, if only through my dreams . . .

I am blessed to have acquaintance with a number of interesting individuals with divergent political, social, religious, and economic backgrounds and opinions. So, I'd taken a couple of weeks off to spend some time with these interesting individuals—to fish a little, play and write some music, drink some beer, and reflect on my life's experiences. To try to make some sense of it all, including why my big-picture idea of the world seemed to be getting fuzzy, and why my *regret* dream seemed to be getting more vivid and more frequent. To try to figure out why, on a number of fronts, my worldview was becoming disorganized, and why there seemed to be so much polarity among people that reasonable social and political discourse seemed to be falling apart.

I had decided to take the bull by the horns and email some of my thoughts to four of my former college professors, who I knew still had their regular Thursday night poker game and drink-a-thon at Saint John's University, in the deep recesses of the Great Hall. You know the place—looks like it came right out of the factory with Earth itself, with heavy old brick and a deep musty scent of history.

What I got back was not at all what I'd hoped for, though I later realized it was exactly what I needed. I could see those four snickering through plumes of cigar smoke as they created a tidy little response that, at least initially, irritated much more than enlightened. As I read it, a voice in my head rang, "Give me five thousand words, single spaced, MLA format by next Tuesday." After shaking off that disgusting thought, I realized that they had precisely summarized the rantings of my addled brain into three distinct categories of subject/predicate.

They didn't answer my query. Better yet, they figured: coalesce my thoughts to allow me to do it myself. *Omne trium perfectum*, the rule of three, the holy Trinity, the cosmic triple, the rule of thirds: was it intentional on their part or just coincidental that they gave me three categories to work with?

The Marines have widely utilized the rule of three, recognizing the maxim that most men can only keep track of three things at once. I'd run across enough guys where that meant penis, beer, penis, but hopefully they were giving me more credit than that.

Their response read:

I) Individual Responsibility vis-à-vis The Role of Big Government.

II) Passing Judgment vis-à-vis Societal Expectation.

III)The Dialogue of Conflict vis-à-vis Political Correctness.

Christ! What kind of heavy shit had I gotten myself into? I'd taken a couple weeks off to clear my head, and now I had opened myself up to the equivalent of a college seminar course from hell.

Wait, wait, wait, *wait*! The good news was that my vacation was just beginning and I could *choose* what I wanted to think about, what to do, and where to go. Right . . .

I was never much into poetry, Scots language, or Robert Burns, but my "best laid schemes" had gone awry and were apparently about to end with me becoming part of the grillwork of a Mack truck.

Chapter 3

Summoning every ounce of strength I could muster, I rapidly jerked the wheel of the Stang to the right and reflexively closed my eyes for the impending crash.

I could hear the Mack's horn blowing uselessly, as if there was a choice in my crossing the center line. As I braced for the massive crash that never came, I was certain I heard a small scraping sound—at which point my eyes re-opened to the sight of the Stang whipping rightward back across the highway.

Knowing the car's characteristics was a plus, as I used a combination of steering and braking to get the Stang to the right shoulder of the road. Releasing another long sigh, I sat there with my hands gripping the wheel until my heart rate slowed down long enough to get the feeling of its beating out of my throat.

Opening the car door, I stepped out to survey the situation. The driver's front tire was completely flat and slightly warped. The chrome front bumper, on close inspection, had a small but deep linear scratch on the outside edge. *One inch further*, I thought, *and the contact would have spun me out of control.* The Mack was long gone.

Sitting back down in the driver's seat, I took out my iPhone and pulled up towing services in Saint Cloud. I was about five miles out of town and would have changed the tire myself, but I wanted to get the Stang up on the rack and get a good look at the front end and suspension before proceeding further north.

The truck from Frank's Garage and Towing arrived within thirty minutes of my phone call, and we had the car in town and up on the rack in another thirty minutes.

On the way into town, I looked over at Frank, whose ripped, greasy bib overalls every bit fit the stereotype most people associate with a mechanic. Generally, I get along very well with mechanics, and I appreciate the hell out of guys who make a living using their hands. One of my friends, a former patient from my primary-care days, is my mechanic. Stan trusts me to use his shop whenever I need to make a repair that he is too busy to do right away himself.

Frank, looking at the car and then looking at me and my non-callused hands, apparently figured I couldn't tell a pipe wrench from a pair of pliers.

"*You* want to get this thing up on the rack and take a look at the front end?" he said, with a hint of disdain.

"Yes, I do," I answered very matter-of-factly. After enough experience in life with enough people, most of us develop some sense of when to get pissed off and aggressive, and when to hold off and assess the situation first. Here I chose the latter. Frank didn't know anything about me and made his own assumptions, and that was his problem.

As it was, I would much rather deal with him any day than with passive-aggressive types, whose numbers, unfortunately, seem to be multiplying. Solid communication between humans these days is difficult enough without adding extra variables. For some reason, that thought, and my interaction with Frank, triggered a nagging memory in the back of my brain. As we drove along, I responded by trying to remember the details of an incident that had happened while I was at St. John's—an incident involving a misunderstanding between another student and myself. I closed my eyes and tried to recall his name, but couldn't.

"We're here, chief," Frank bellowed, yanking me out of my reverie as we pulled up next to his shop. When we had the car up on the rack, and Frank was removing the flat, I started inspecting the power steering and front suspension. "Control valve looks brand new," growled Frank after he pulled off the flat tire.

"The front end kept shuddering after I installed the first one—a remake," I said, naming a well-known parts supplier that had sent me the unit. "So, I managed to track down a rebuilt OEM control valve and steering rack, and did an R & R." OEM stood for original equipment manufacturer, and R & R meant "remove and replace."

"Seems fine now," I said.

"I had the same problem with units from that company," said Frank, apparently convinced by now that I knew which end of a hammer to hang on to. "Here—come take a look at your tire. These are incredibly well-built tires, and I'm going to guess these have only a couple hundred miles on them, right?"

"Right."

"Well, something, or someone, put about a three-inch slit on the inside of this tire, shallow enough to not flatten it, but deep enough for it to give way under highway conditions. There aren't any other marks on the tire, just a clean cut. Where I come from, we'd wonder more about a some*one* than a some*thing*."

With the spare now installed, and the front end, the other tires, and the brake lines inspected, I again pointed the Stang north. Frank and I had traded a few stories first and we shook hands when I left. It turns out Frank was somewhat of a Mustang fanatic himself, so we had been able to converse about the finer points of keeping these old classics on the road. After paying the bill, I had tipped him well for his prompt service. He kept the tire and told me that he would have a friend who "knew about such things" take a look at it.

Back on the highway, I tried to concentrate on my driving, but now I had another issue to deal with. I was certain that my new tire hadn't contacted any sort of road hazard. It was far less certain that there wasn't contact from some other form of hazard. Trying to concentrate on my driving, I racked my brain as to who might have it in for me enough to slit my tire—assuming Frank was correct. It was too much for me to fathom right at that point, so I decided to stay vigilant and wait to hear back from Frank.

Within a few hours, I had made it to the town of Walker and its incredible views of Leech Lake. I stopped at the local Super One at the edge of town to grab some groceries for camp and jumped back on the highway.

Later, as I pulled into camp, I saw seven men positioned in a circle around a fire ring that spewed a four-foot-high flame—hot enough to instantly separate them from their eyebrows if they ventured closer than three feet. Five had beers, one had a rum and Coke, and the other was finishing off an orange soda. All were seated in green plastic lawn chairs, two of those strained to the breaking point as large bodies pressed against their flimsy backs. I was informed later that another one of those flimsy backs had given way, and shortly thereafter the flame had temporarily risen to six feet.

Schmitty, poking at the fire with a long shillelagh he had carved himself, told me later that, just as I was driving in, the banter among them had started with him. "Where the hell is Doc?"

"He's not exactly known for his punctuality," observed Steve.

"Or his penmanship," offered Jake.

"Both of which catapulted him into medical school," replied Dustin.

Schmitty's father, Gus, and brother-in-law, Dan, erupted with throaty laughs, and his brother, Mike, had added, "Here comes the SOB now."

I had turned off the main road and guided the Stang down the winding gravel trail that led to camp. Along either side, pine trees of various sizes and shapes marked the border of the trail. I cranked down the window and took a good whiff. The smell of Christmas instantly relaxed me. Pine scent has always been some sort of olfactory endorphin for me and never ceases to take me back to a wonderfully calm place—to the most incredible of all holidays.

Seeing the guys seated around the fire as I drove up, I reminded myself that I'd decided not to tell them about what had happened to my tire—at least until I had more information. Besides, I knew it wouldn't be long before the trash talk began, as would be expected, and welcomed, from a bunch of really good friends.

"Schmitty" was really Bill Schmidt, and he and Mike were both from my hometown. Mike and his wife had escaped Minnesota by moving south many years previous, but he relished the opportunities to get back and let his hair down with the boys. He was funnier than hell, and you had no idea what he was going to say next, especially when rum was involved.

Schmitty and I hung out a lot together, especially since his divorce. He was a big man, and the kind of guy who would literally give you the shirt off of his back, presuming the divorce hadn't already taken it. Jake was his son, and Dustin McKenna was his soon-to-be son-in-law, both going to the same school as Jake's sister (and Dustin's fiancée), Audrey. Missing was Dan's wife, Beth, who often made the trip and who always made incredible meals.

Steve was also a long-term great friend, whom I had met, of all places, in the church choir. It had taken all of about ten minutes for us to realize that our common bond would be our guitars and irreverence. If the punishment for irreverence via music played in the choir loft (even in the corner at low volume) is a one-way ticket to hell, then I need to invest in some asbestos shoes pronto. Unless God has a really good sense of humor, he or she likely was not amused by our blues-riff-laden "You've got to change your evil ways—Jesus." Initially, I thought Steve's wife, Ann, who sang with us in the choir, was similarly not amused. Actually, I wondered if she had some sort of ophthalmic disorder—*too bad*, I thought, *a woman with a voice that incredible who just can't seem to stop rolling her eyes.*

We didn't improve our cause any more a few years later when we decided to shake up the church ladies by re-enacting a Bing Crosby Christmas movie. We spontaneously showed up at the parish basement for the church ladies' Christmas party dressed as the Haynes girls and did a version of "Sisters," complete with leg garters, tutus, and blue feather fans. A single video copy of that event is held under lock and key, its revelation guarded by Pentagon-like security. It is referred to only in our ice fishing shack on Carl's Lake—when our defenses have been lowered by friend Bruce's flask of bourbon.

Steve, a stellar golfer, had tried fairly patiently over the years to turn me into a decent golfer. In this endeavor, I was the poster child for the adage that you can't succeed at everything. I'd always told myself that if I managed to find the time to hit the links more than two or three times a year that things would be different, but I'm not sure. I was always a damn good softball player, but I'm not sure that my brain ever completely separated the two sports. Steve eventually just let me hack away, and enjoyed standing back behind the tee box whispering to the two other golfers we'd been paired with: "Watch this guy's swing—you'll never believe he's a doctor."

Jake and Dustin had made the trip up from college to join the entourage along with Gus, who had owned the place for years. Gus was a former Marine with a heart of gold and a thundering velvet demeanor—a man to whom Schmitty had ascribed his own steadfastness by learning as a child that "perfect is good enough." I had known Gus and his wife, Helen, since I was a kid. Some of my most cherished memories are those of Christmas Eves at their house during college and med school, when I would come back for mass at Saint James. We'd sing up a storm for the service, then head toward their place—braving the bite of frigid air and crunching over frozen snow as we made our way past brightly lit thirty-foot pine trees.

I parked the car and made my way toward the fire. "I didn't know you were bringing the Stang," said Schmitty.

"I didn't either," I said. "Last-minute decision."

Schmitty winked. "See any little green men on the way up?"

"Very funny," I countered.

"Though I suppose *they* could have been responsible for the legs missing on those rotisserie chickens you brought us the last time," he added.

"You make one mistake and it sticks with you forever," I laughed. My snacking habits were legendary, and these guys never let me forget it. Of course they were right, and if it weren't for a pair of running shoes my body habitus would be legendary—on the order of Orson Welles.

I plopped down in a plastic chair and Steve handed me a beer and a bowl of Schmitty's homemade chili. In the annals of legend, Steve took the distinction for beer drinking. Everyone around this fire got chided, in their own hilarious way, by everyone else. Steve's comeuppance was generally a "stern" warning from Gus, who at the rare times he caught Steve without a beer handed him one, with the reprimand "You're out of uniform, soldier."

"The day's moving along, and we're ready to get out on the water," said Schmitty. "You ready, Doc?"

"You guys have waited for me long enough already," I said. "I need to walk around, stretch my legs, breathe some of this incredible air, and contemplate nature for a bit. Why don't you head out, and I'll jump in on the next round."

"Sounds good, mon," Schmitty replied. "Let's ditty bop down to the boat landing and make acquaintance with some fish, boys. Doc can do his Thoreau thing and we'll all meet up later."

"I'll stick around the fire and put it out if you aren't back in a couple of hours," Gus added.

We all walked down the road toward the boat landing together. Schmitty had, of course, already stocked two boats with gear and coolers full of drinks and snacks.

I waved good-bye to the guys as they split off toward the landing, and I continued walking down the old logging road that ran alongside the woods. The woods were, in fact, a heavy pine stand that had in recent years been designated a state forest. The air was fresh, the smells were clean, and noise was absent—a perfect brain canvas for unencumbered wandering thought. In my backpack, among other things, were a pair of binoculars, one of my favorite books on North Woods birds, and of course a few snacks.

I ambled to the end of the logging road where it cut into the woods. Arriving there, I stepped off of the road and slowly worked my way into the woods, enjoying the incredible solitude afforded me. I came across a small stream that meandered through the trees, bubbling its way down toward the lake. Looking closely at its edge, I was surprised to see what on closer inspection turned out to be Equisetum. Ever since my days in college, I had been fascinated by this primitive vascular plant, believed to be one of the oldest plants to still exist on earth. The Greeks and Romans supposedly used the plant medicinally, as did American colonists. It got tagged with the nickname "horsetail," because it literally resembles that structure. I had seen it on a number of creek bed edges in the southern part of the state, but never this far north.

Walking on, I let my mind wander off to a couple of its favorite preoccupations, music and medicine.

As with golf, I had often wondered whether devoting

more time to practice would improve my technique—when playing the guitar. Granted, in comparison I was a much better guitar player than I was a golfer, but I knew that there was still much left to be desired. Of all the musicians I'd ever met or worked with, I'd only met two who were willing to say that they were really good at what they did. They all knew that right down the street, there was someone who might be considered by someone else to have a better style, or a better voice, or better technique. So they labored on to perfect their craft.

It's not exactly the same way in medicine. Not to say that all doctors out there are running around with big egos, but their numbers on a percentage basis certainly outnumber musicians. To a degree I understand it, especially in certain specialties. Just like state troopers, certain physicians face emergent situations on a regular basis, and therefore need to keep their guard up. I respect the need in both situations.

I won't, however, give carte blanche to *anyone* in *all* situations. That especially includes bloviating undereducated celebrities, and anyone else who thinks that possessing gobs of money entitles them to exhibit unbridled snooty behavior.

That thought has crossed my mind often over the years, when I realize that I, too, could've chosen to try to lick my way up the corporate ladder, or try to sell myself up the entertainment industry ladder. Both are tough hauls, with not many making it to the top. Therefore, I don't begrudge those making $20 million a movie, or $1 million a year as a CEO. I do, however, begrudge those who vilify the corporate exec's salary while simultaneously drooling over the entertainer. I am also quite fatigued with being reminded by the $20-million-a-movie crowd that I personally am not doing enough to *save the whales.* Call me terrible, or call me a guy who's just trying to figure it out.

I do know that each of us eventually decides—by default or otherwise—what it is that we concentrate on most in our lives. The ability to make those kinds of choices is the beauty of living in America. I'm amused, however, that in some quarters there appears to be the impression that there is a set of experiential cultural basics that we all must achieve, lest we be labeled culturally inept. Some likely view me that way because I'm largely in the dark when they reference parts of many of the movies made in the past twenty years.

I'm obviously better with music, but not all of it. I once ran into a guy while on vacation who waited all of about fourteen seconds before launching into the story of how he wrote a song that sold over two million copies—and then got agitated when I couldn't immediately recall his ten-year-old effort. Sorry—I must have been busy doing something relatively unimportant, like CPR.

My phone rang just then, and I hit the answer button to hear Schmitty on the other end proclaim: "Just checking to see if your new phone has service up here, Doc."

"Loud and clear," I assured him.

I walked on, recalling that Schmitty—in an attempt to point out that people pay too much attention to bloviating celebrities instead of the real heroes they should respect—once said that he was going to create a website called "Idon'tgiveashit.com." He then accurately realized that it would simply give the issue *more* attention.

Back to the subject of egos, I thought again about medicine, where—like life in general—the presentation of a big ego can often be just a presentation to mask something else. In some cases, however, it may simply be a good coping mechanism. A word to the wise: As long as your surgeon is skilled at what she does, try not to worry about her ego.

In my case, I am happy to be what I consider a skilled diagnostician. I'll admit that I can't recall to you a compendium of every rare disorder, or the technical details behind every drug's function, or recite the latest (and likely to be trumped next month) study on cholesterol management. These are the reasons why I now practice emergency medicine—to use my skills as a diagnostician. My personal goal as a physician is to maintain and, whenever possible, enhance those skills.

I wandered on, marinating the thoughts of musicianship and medical diagnoses in my mind, and reflecting on my life in general. I was so engrossed in the marinating that I walked right into a huge pine tree—huge for a pine, being well over two feet across. Fortunately I walked into the side that I did, because as I walked around it I noticed that the opposite side had a wooden ladder nailed to it. My eyes followed the ladder up the tree to a seat made out of two-by-four boards. *Deer hunting stand*, I thought, and wondered what the view looked like from twenty feet up.

I crawled up the ladder and plopped down on the seat. Removing my backpack, I placed it on the boards next to me, front facing as always. I released a deep sigh and looked out across the woods. *Pretty much the same view as from the ground*, I thought, as I bent my neck completely back and took a deep breath, still marinating on music and medicine.

What happened in the next few moments remains fuzzy at best. I had reopened my eyes to what essentially looked like a swirling cloud of blue-green gas—a cloud that I appeared to be in the middle of. Everything was floating—me, the cloud, my thoughts . . . I somehow felt that my own presence was *expanded*—my head felt huge, but my entire psyche was experiencing a type of tranquility that defies any explanation. I reached out, moving my arms in all directions, and couldn't feel anything. I knew that I wasn't hearing anything, but in my mind, music was playing—music that also defied explanation. The closest I could later come to defining anything like the music that was playing in my mind was the old Eric Burdon tune "Spill the Wine." I didn't do drugs, but that song always made me feel like I had taken something that made me float.

Floating I was, with no concept of space or time during the entire experience. Sometime during it, however, I looked down between my legs and saw myself sitting in a tree stand, head back, backpack next to me. I remember an incredible feeling of warmth, inside me and all around me.

I recall reverting back to my standard process of trying to figure out anything—deductive reasoning—and the more I tried, the more I realized the futility of what I was doing. Deductive reasoning initially requires the separation of entities in order to eventually arrive at a conclusion. In the place I was, there was no ability to separate anything. Everything, including me—again in an indescribable way—felt completely interconnected.

As confusing or unnerving as it should have been, or could have been, I didn't really feel confused or on edge. Despite not really understanding what was happening, I felt a peace building inside of me that I had never felt before—kind of a biofeedback progressive muscle relaxation *on steroids*, where I eventually moved toward total peace and absolutely nothing else, except total interconnection to everyone and everything.

As I built toward that feeling of total peace, I realized that the blue-green cloud that I was in appeared to be thinning out. Images of my life began racing past me, too fast to focus on—kind of like a movie being played at ten times its normal speed. As I desperately tried to focus on them, I realized that the more I allowed myself to relax into the total peace state, the clearer the images became.

I also became aware that the peace state was not a state devoid of emotion. However, the emotions I felt were bathed in tranquility, yet sharply defined, unlike all of those fuzzy-edged "feelings" I had experienced during my life that we have labeled "emotions." As this happened, I remember suddenly and completely understanding the difference between two distinct emotions—a difference that I realized had been eluding me and, I would suspect, a large part of humanity—based on some of society's behaviors.

Those emotions were compassion and empathy—feelings described by two words that unfortunately had been used interchangeably by many in trying to express them.

Indeed, both did involve the awakening of an awareness to something, or especially to someone. The true *emotion* of empathy, I suddenly realized, stopped right there. Compassion, on the other hand, went far beyond that point, to the much deeper sense of sharing the needs or the suffering of another individual or group, and in that sharing, to be inclined to give support to them. That concept became even further defined by the *interconnectedness* I was feeling, as I began to grasp what the true concept of support meant to interconnected beings, well beyond the material aid that human beings patted themselves on the back for supplying to others.

As my life images became clearer, I felt a tremendous desire to view and recall them, and to do so with my awakening sense of true emotion. As I was beginning to visualize them, my sense of utter tranquility suddenly was pierced by a full-on rush of dread. Images flew past of a man who appeared to be carrying some kind of container in each hand as he crept along in the darkness, followed by the foggy outline of another man who appeared to be crouched in a clump of trees with a rifle.

As I tried to hone in on the images, I felt a sudden surge—a rush of something passing through my body. The surge felt like a large release of energy as the sensation of my body floating passed and was replaced with a sensation of heaviness. I became aware of something in the background that I was actually hearing, not something playing in my brain. By the time the floating sensation was completely replaced with that of heaviness, I realized that what I was hearing was my cell phone ringing . . .

"You there?" came the voice from the other end.

I was trying to open my eyes, and somehow eventually muttered, "Mmmm."

"Doc, you there?" came the voice again, and more mumbling from me.

"Derek!" yelled the voice from the other end. This time I woke up.

"Are you okay, man? Sounds like you're having a stroke or something."

"No, I'm okay. Must have drifted off to sleep in the tree stand I'm sitting in."

"All righty then. We're motoring the boat back toward camp. See you soon."

"Okay," I said, as I shook my head to clear the cobwebs.

As I did so, I briefly recalled another image from near the end of my visions. It was an image in which I was being observed from far away by an unknown man during the entire time I was in the cloud—a man who had decided that he would only smile again when my respiratory rate had reached zero . . .

Chapter 4

I grabbed my backpack and slowly extricated myself from the tree by crawling backwards down the rungs of the ladder of the tree stand. Leaning back against the big pine, I closed my eyes and rubbed my temples. I slowly opened my eyes, wondering if I would wake up in the familiar surroundings of my bedroom and realize that I had dreamt what had just transpired.

No such luck. Not that I didn't find the experience interesting, but how it ended left me extremely confused, and I needed to sort out what had just happened. My body also felt so *heavy* that I honestly wasn't sure that I could crawl back up into the tree and try to repeat the experience, though I did have a sudden strong desire to attempt to recall and review every event in my life that I could . . .

Pushing my body away from the tree, I began walking back the way I had come. I weaved my way down the trail from the big pine toward the old logging road that led back to camp. "Weaved" was definitely the operative word. My body felt like a hot air balloon, with the basket being everything from my neck on down. My giant balloon head felt like it was swaying in the breeze, somehow barely escaping impalement by the towering pines I was passing under.

I stumbled onto the logging trail and walked as slowly as I could, hoping the funk I was in would begin to abate by the time I reached camp. Clumps of thick green moss lined most of the left edge of the trail, which bordered the deeper woods. I walked on that side, taking advantage of the softness and quietness it afforded.

That serenity was breached by my first step off of the trail onto the gravel camp driveway, with a deafening crunch that seem to travel from my heel up the back of my legs, through my spine, and out the top of my skull. I slowed down even more and realized that the balloon seemed to slowly be deflating, and my overactive senses seemed to be calming down. By the time I walked into camp, I had closed back in on normality. Opening the trunk of the Mustang, I dropped in the backpack.

I had no idea what had happened in that tree, but I knew myself well enough to know that the only way to try to make any sense of it was through the usual deep introspection that I generally employed whenever something totally baffled me. Fortunately, that didn't happen very often, but I dreaded the hollow feeling that accompanied it when it did. The hollow feeling, I discovered a few years back, was related to the self-flagellation I usually put myself through when the introspection was about an interpersonal issue, as I realized that I usually start out my thought process on such issues by beating up on myself first.

I slunk into the garage, opened the fridge, grabbed a beer, and began walking out around the garage down toward the stream that bordered the back side of camp. I desperately needed to sit down somewhere and begin my introspection—the repeated replay of the events of the afternoon.

"Hey, Doc," came a yell from the hillside. "Look at this haul!" I turned around and watched the troops come up over the top of the hillside. Schmitty and Jake each had a stringer with two good-sized northern pike, and Dustin and Steve were close behind, each with a nice walleye. Mike and Dan brought up the rear, carrying a cooler. I surmised that Gus must have still been in the bunkhouse finishing off a long nap, while the rest of the crew had taken both boats out for an apparently successful fishing excursion.

"Get rid of me and your luck always improves," I yelled back.

"You okay?" Schmitty asked as they approached me. "You look kind of pale."

"I'll tell you about it later," I said, realizing that I was not going to get to do my loner routine and sneak off for a round of mental masturbation.

"All right, mon," he said. "Fire up the fryer and grab that box of Fry Magic, dudes, while I clean these bad boys."

In no time, we were standing around huge wooden wire spools that acted as tables, beers in hand, eating incredibly delicious fresh fish. "Don't they feed you in Saint Louis?" Schmitty chided Mike, as he wolfed down his fourth helping.

"Not like this they don't," uttered Mike through a mouthful of walleye.

"*Chew* that fish, Mike," I said. "Do you have a problem with mastication?"

Mike looked at me and smiled. "Listen, Doc, what I do in the privacy of my own home is no one's business but mine."

Gus made sure that we had everything shipshape clean before we walked the one hundred feet down to the fire pit. Jake was already there with a garden hose, watering down about a thirty-foot perimeter of grass around the area. I thought about how meticulous these guys were with everything they did, especially when it came to safety. Gus may have been a bit staunch with the "Marine" routine at times, but it had probably paid off more times than anyone had ever known.

We carried our plastic chairs with us as we went. Jake and Dustin had already hauled a wheelbarrow full of split wood down to the metal fire ring and were stacking it in place inside the ring, preparing it to be lit. I pulled Schmitty aside. "I need to talk to you about something."

"Shoot," he said.

"This isn't easy for me, buddy," I began. I paused for what seemed like an eternity, and then added: "I had a really weird experience when I was in the woods this afternoon."

He cocked his head. "Did you have your hand in your pants again?"

"Wish it was that simple," I said, in a tone serious enough for him to make a remark.

"Let's walk up to the garage and get a beer."

We grabbed beers out of the fridge and sat down. I recounted to him my experience, minus the confusing images at the end. When I finished, I said: "I'm telling you man, you know me and I'm a pretty straight shooter, but this thing rattled me. It was so weird that I started to wonder whether you had reverted back to your old days and put some 'shrooms in the chili."

"Now that would've been a way to liven up the party," he laughed. "Too bad I didn't think of it . . . or did I?" He completely ignored the quizzical look I threw at him and took a swig of his beer. "This 'thing' you were in—how would you describe it again?"

"I don't know what the hell to call it," I muttered. "Some sort of . . . vortex . . . I guess. A kind of whirling, swirling . . . vortex."

"How did you get into it again?" he asked.

"I was thinking about that as I walked back to camp," I said, "trying to remember exactly what I did in that tree stand when it happened. I do remember tipping my head back as far as it would go, so it ended up being stuck out a bit behind the tree stand, and that's when I seemed to be in the . . . vortex. That's not all of it. I felt like I was floating and had this utter sense of tranquility. My life was being played before my eyes, and I was just beginning to be able to visualize it when your call came in."

"Jesus, man, that almost sounds like a near-death experience." Schmitty scratched his beard. "So, either the vortex was in a place that you had to bend your head to reach, or bending your head back that far made you feel that you were in the vortex."

He took another swig. "I'm going to play doctor here, and not even charge you a fortune for the consult. Let's say that just bending your head back was what made you feel that you were in a vortex. I had an uncle who had something like this, and you guys have a name for it . . . something like . . . vertebro base something or other."

"Not textbook symptoms for it, but . . . vertebrobasilar insufficiency," I said, matter-of-factly.

"Right, another one of those $10,000 words—literally," he muttered. "Like you would know shit from Shinola if you ever stepped into a power plant."

"Whoa, man," I tossed back. Being the friends we were, we rarely got in a tussle about anything. In fact, we could kid each other about just about anything and never worry that we were stepping on anything sensitive. My problem was there were certain things about being a physician that I was sensitive about, like money, and unfortunately I would sometimes forget who I was having the dialogue with.

Schmitty enjoyed his "good old boy" act but indeed was one of the most well-informed and well-rounded people I'd ever met. After viewing the paintings he had done and kept hidden in his basement, I told him that I would make certain that his greatness would be known posthumously. He assured me that that would never happen, only because I would never outlive him.

"You know exactly how I feel about you," I said. "I suspect without a doubt that you are smarter than I am, and I know for certain that you are better-read."

He glared at me for about five seconds, then burst out laughing. "That's a fact, Jack, and don't you forget it."

I tried to glare back at him, but only lasted about three seconds before I burst out laughing as well. "Let's get down to the fire," he said.

By then it was starting to get dark, and nature was about to put on its show. I was more than ready for a relaxed night around the fire when my cell phone rang. I looked at the number and got one of those sinking feelings I occasionally got when I was in primary care and delivered babies.

Not that I disliked delivering babies—I loved it. Those days, nothing made me feel more like a real doctor than assisting a new life into the world. Babies of course never came at "convenient" times for the expecting parents or their doctors, but sometimes the timing was downright terrible. As family physicians, we almost always delivered our own OB patients, even if we weren't on call. So, theoretically, you could work all day in the clinic, be on call that night for admissions, work the next day, and then hopefully have a night off. What often happened was that that "night off" ended up becoming a "night on" when the call from OB came in, which could sometimes keep us up all night. For me, mixed in were the occasional overnight moonlighting stints I did to help pay the bills, especially the massive student loans. One memorable week, the stars completely misaligned, and those stellar events occurred back to back to back. The result was a stretch where I worked fifty-four hours straight without any real sleep until I got a break for a small nap—not an event that I, nor anyone else, should ever try to replicate.

It wasn't that we weren't busy enough in the clinic to make money—we worked our butts off. However, being in a private, noncorporate-connected clinic that was "too close" to a metro area, we had been reduced to precious little contracting clout with the insurance industry. They really didn't care if we disappeared, or if our patients had to drive several miles in other directions to another clinic where doctors accepted their insurance. The industry played this little game with everyone, and as privately owned clinics began to disappear, the number of cards in their hand only increased.

Eventually, the reimbursements they offered us were so poor that we were, for the same work, taking home barely above half of what doctors were being paid who worked in corporate clinics. So, we worked harder and we worked longer to try to make up the difference. We weren't greedy, but everyone has bills to pay—in many of our cases jacked sky-high by student loans—and of course everyone would eventually like to own a nice house, drive a decent car, help their kids through college, and try to put some money away for retirement.

In a private clinic, there were no paid vacations, which meant that when you weren't there, you weren't getting paid. And there were no paid pension plans. Thus, we worked harder and accepted less for the privilege of continuing to get to see the patients we knew and cared for—and for the privilege of lesser clinical interference from the insurance industry.

As all "good" things must come to an end, so did "less clinical interference from the insurance industry." Seeing our patients and taking care of them in the way we saw fit as physicians made working a lot harder for less money tolerable. The end of the tolerance came when the puppet master had managed to attach so many strings that the regular ethical practice of medicine became unsustainable. My group, and a lot of other family physicians, finally just gave up trying to keep the doors open.

The phone call, of course, was not from OB, but it was from the emergency department. They knew I was on vacation, so they obviously weren't calling because I had missed a shift. Sometimes the staff or other doctors called to clarify an order or a chart note, so I punched *answer* and said hello. Within fifteen seconds, I knew it would be a short night for me around the fire, as I would be getting up at about 5 a.m. to drive back south and cover the day shift tomorrow, a shift that had been left open and essentially uncoverable due to the ravaging of the staff by a rampant gastrointestinal virus. I muttered something about not wanting to drive the Mustang back unless it was absolutely daylight, and Schmitty, ever generous, told me to take his old Blazer instead.

We pulled up the plastic chairs in a circle around the fire that Jake and Dustin had started. At the time it was only two feet high, but as I knew, it was yet in its infancy. The stars were beginning to pop out overhead, and a light breeze was cooling down the warm day. The fire felt warm and inviting and primal. We were all beginning to enter into a relaxation phase borne of a few beers and the redistribution of blood away from our brains and extremities toward GI tracts faced with the digestion of ten pounds of fried fish. I, for one, didn't mind the blood being directed away from my cranium, as I welcomed the damper it put on my racing thoughts about the vortex.

At camp, we all loved this time of day. Time to tell jokes and share stories, including, of course, the tale of the big one that got away that day on the lake. I suspected that the conversation was similar around other campfires in the state. Our conversations, however, always moved far beyond this type of banter—which was one of the reasons I absolutely loved coming up here.

Campfire dialogue at Bern Lake followed its own rubric, and usually made me feel like I was in the middle of an episode of the old TV series *Northern Exposure.* As much as I hate the idea of stereotyping the subjects we *should* have been talking about, the idea of a bunch of modern men who hadn't showered in three days sitting around a campfire discussing ancient civilizations and world affairs conjured up its own brand of anachronism.

That night's conversation quickly went from the home-brewed beer we were enjoying on to its ties to the ancient Sumerians. Steve and his wife, Ann, both enjoyed excellent wines, and Ann, as a result of her restaurant job, had gained her sommelier certification recently. She and Steve—what a shock—also enjoyed sampling various beers, and somehow this led the three of us to Vine Park Brewing Company in Saint Paul, where we whipped up several tasty varieties of beer and wine, some of which we decided to enjoy that night.

"I read something recently that solidifies the importance of beer to mankind," said Schmitty.

"Is a justification really necessary?" replied Steve.

"Of course not," noted Schmitty, "but you might be interested in this, especially since the original article was in the *Chicago Tribune*—and was reprinted by the Minneapolis *Star Tribune*."

"If you are talking about the article about the ancient Sumerians," I said, "I saw that one, too."

"That's the one," said Schmitty. He went on. "What is now Iraq used to be occupied by the Sumerians—amazing people—inscribed their cuneiform language on clay tablets. Know what was repeatedly mentioned on those tablets? Beer! This civilization was one of the first to record their thoughts in writing, which gave us an insight into the tremendous development of their knowledge in things like mathematics and law—really a group that created the concept of civilization. Turns out that they were brewing beer for thousands of years before they ever started writing."

"So," I added, "per the article, a branch of the University of Chicago—the Oriental Institute—apparently decided it was important to re-create Sumerian beer."

Gus elbowed Steve. "Guess we'll have to get you on a plane to the old hometown as soon as possible," he laughed.

"We studied the Sumerians in an ancient world civilization course I took last semester," said Jake.

"I was in the same class," said Dustin, and added, "the Oriental Institute in Chicago actually has an exact replica of the Code of Hammurabi."

"Something to make up for the shortcomings of their pro football team?" drawled Dan, shooting a look at Steve.

"Let me see," Steve mused, "when did the Minnesota Vikings last win a Super Bowl? And let's see . . . the Bears, the Bears—oh yeah, the 1985 Bears."

"Apparently last year's Christmas gift didn't teach you anything," I said. Tiring of hearing 1985 Bears references from Steve, I had given him copies of the Bears doing "The Super Bowl Shuffle" on all available media at the time—vinyl, cassette tape, and VHS tape—in an effort to lend him the realization of the passage of time. It was totally ineffective.

"Anyway," continued Dustin, "in class, the Code of Hammurabi brought forth a very interesting discussion of ancient ethics compared to the modern world."

"So, as *I* remember," said Mike, "Hammurabi's code was an ancient legal code."

"That's right," replied Jake. "It essentially prescribed an appropriate counter punishment for an offense—using the exact reciprocity principle."

"At least I know he's going to class," said Schmitty.

"An eye for an eye, and a tooth for a tooth, right?" said Mike.

"That's right," said Jake, adding, "the discussion got pretty heated."

"How's that?" I asked, thinking about my experience in the vortex earlier that day.

"Well," said Jake, "everyone pretty well agreed that the concept of an eye for an eye had no place in modern society—though it did engender a round of discussion about the death penalty. What ended up getting heated was the general discussion about deterrence for any kind of behavior, especially as it relates to what society is expected to provide to those who don't seem to want to exercise responsibility for themselves."

I decided this was the time to show the group the communication I had received from my college professors.

"Looks like you stepped into it with both feet," laughed Schmitty.

"Indeed I did," I said, "and I'm really interested in getting opinions from everyone here about it, but since I now have to be up at 5 a.m., I'll let it marinate with you guys, and hopefully we can talk about it when I come back up."

I got nods of approval as Steve came walking back to the fire with two guitars. I took a guitar from Steve and said to the group, "Grabbing this guitar and thinking about that communication from my professors reminds me of an experience I had playing with my rock band at a wedding a few years back. It was the old 'content versus intent' thing, which I expect we may run into a bit as we discuss that communication."

"How's that?" asked Gus.

"This story actually explains it pretty well," I said. "We were asked to play for this newly married couple's wedding dance, and we had shown her our song list, which she said she was quite happy with. As these things go, a few days before the dance she asked us to learn a new song that we had never played before that she wanted to sing to her new husband at the dance. There really wasn't time to learn the new song, which was just as well with us, but we agreed to play her CD through the sound system so she could sing the song. She wanted to do it before the dance actually started, so we all pulled up a chair and listened to her sing "I Don't Know How to Love Him" from *Jesus Christ Superstar*. It's a beautiful song and she sang it very well, but we all turned our heads a bit when she perfectly belted out *all* of the lyrics, including the lines: 'And I've had so many men before, in very many ways, he's just one more.' Now, I don't know if this rendition of the song had anything to do with it, but I'm not certain that the marriage survived."

Around a rip-roaring fire, and under a totally clear and beautiful starry sky, we plucked out a few old standards and a few rock 'n' roll tunes before we started playing some slow blues riffs.

"God, I love this stuff. What the hell happened to *music*?" asked Dustin.

"Nothing," replied Schmitty. "We can still listen to the *good* stuff."

The guys, except Gus, chimed in from time to time with the vocals until Steve finally asked him: "Are you musically inclined, Gus?"

"Musically inclined?" he answered. "I can barely play the radio." He chuckled. "Hell, to you guys, Earth, Wind and Fire is a band. To me, they were the only three elements we knew about when I was in high school."

Steve laughed and put his guitar down to grab a beer. I kept plucking away.

A few minutes later Dan piped up, "Hey Doc, what's the name of the song again that you wrote about your brother-in-law?"

"I remember it," offered Steve. "I haven't heard from him in a little while. How are he and your sister doing?"

"Living the dream in Colorado, he says."

"Is he still doing information technology?"

"Yes he is, and he still insists that IT is the only place in the universe where immutable laws of physics are regularly broken."

"How's that?" Dan asked.

"He says he still hasn't seen any other place where shit can run uphill and downhill at the same time."

"Guess I volunteered for that one," laughed Dan. "But what about the song?"

"It's not so much about him as it is about one of his sayings that I took and ran with," I answered, "and he has quite a few. I used a couple of them on the album the band recorded, and I'm making sure he gets credit on the album cover when we finally release it. The song you're talking about uses a saying that Vince laughed that he used to use in his dating days before he married my sister Rose. He said he would take out a girl and spend about twenty minutes talking about himself, look at her, and say, 'That's enough talking about me. So, what do *you* think of me?'"

"How'd that work out for him?" laughed Gus.

"Well, he was lucky enough to marry my sister, so he must've stopped using it somewhere along the line."

I played "(You Say) It's All About Me"—starting with the refrain, followed by three verses and a couple more refrains:

> You say it's all about me, you say it's all about me
> You've heard me talk enough about all my stuff
> And all I think about is me—I do agree
> So what do you think of me?
>
> Where I come from it's true, it could be all about you
> 'Round here it's small enough, they'll never call your bluff
> And bein' on top wasn't really too tough
> 'Cause they didn't have a clue
>
> Growing up there was no test—I was way above the rest
> When it came to perfection, I couldn't be nearer
> And it couldn't be clearer when I looked in the mirror
> I was lookin' at the best

There's really nothing to fear, 'cause it's really quite clear
In my small town they really dig me
'Cause round these parts I'm like the tallest pygmy
So just leave me right here

You say it's all about me, you say it's all about me
You've heard me talk enough about all my stuff
And all I think about is me—I do agree
So what do you think of me?
So what do you think of me?
So what do you think of me?

"Man, that's vintage Vince!" laughed Steve.

"Indeed it is," I replied as I headed off to the bunkhouse to get a few hours of sleep, hoping that I could make more sense out of my vortex experience with the coming light of day.

Chapter 5

The drive back to the Twin Cities, fueled by three cups of coffee, was pretty uneventful until I hit the typical northern suburbs traffic. My mind was so wrapped up in trying to sort out my experience in the tree stand that hitting the traffic felt like suddenly driving into a snowstorm. I snaked my way through the downtown congestion, across the Mississippi River bridge, and eventually across the Minnesota River.

Rolling the Blazer into the parking lot, I guided it into a "physicians" parking space. *One of the few perks we have left*, I thought, as I opened the door and grabbed for my backpack. It wasn't there. *Damn*, I thought—*must have left it in the trunk of the Mustang*. I closed the door and started walking toward the ER.

As I walked, I started thinking about how things had changed in medicine. As much as I detest whining, I also detest refusing to face the reality that has come with those changes, like the perception of "perks."

Reality here is that the powers that be have decided that physicians are somehow unable to resist the temptation that comes with any sort of perk—like being offered five dollars worth of free pizza while being given updated information on a new drug that has become available, and then receiving samples that I can use for patients who really need them. That perk is somehow supposed to transform me into the Stepford physician who prescribes the latest expensive cholesterol-lowering medication to every man, woman, and child that walks into my office. I, of course, am not considered to possess the moral fortitude to resist, but I am somehow considered trustworthy enough to walk into an exam room five minutes later by myself and examine a patient wearing nothing but a gown.

Whoa, I thought, as I walked toward the side entrance of the emergency department. *Someone drank a huge cup of cynical this morning.* More accurately, I reconsidered, a cup of truth with some cynical creamer.

Our patients really did appreciate the samples, though, and sometimes even the containers. When Steve got married, the hat I made him out of Viagra boxes apparently went over rather well at the "club" he visited during his bachelor party.

The crunch of gravel under my shoes and the sweet smell of freshly mown grass pulled me out of my funk as I reached the metal entry door. I pulled out my identification badge, swiped it through the card reader, and pulled the door open after I heard the familiar click. My pupils enlarged as my eyes adjusted to the relative darkness of the hallway compared to the bright light outside.

"Hey, Kath—how's it going?" I inquired, as I sauntered into the ER.

"Doughnuts are old, coffee's cold, patients are bold . . . Damn, Doc, sounds like one of your blues songs," she muttered. "By the way, thanks for coming in on short notice *and* during your vacation to fill the open shift."

I moved on down the hall and opened my locker, where I had stored some extra clothes. The smell of rubbing alcohol kicked the hippocampal area of my brain into gear, and a few million neuronal connections made love to each other instantaneously. The result was a vivid recollection of the first time I walked down this same hall and thought about how confusing and disorganized the place looked—probably the same way it looked to anyone who set eyes on it the first time. Amazing what a few years of working in the same place does to create familiarity with chaos.

I took a quick shower, slipped into a pair of scrubs, wrapped a stethoscope over my neck, and grabbed my name tag to clip it on. I liked the face that stared back at me, probably the only name tag picture I'd ever seen that actually looked better than its owner.

"Hey, Doc, we got a full house out here. Get your face outta the doughnuts."

"I love you too, Kath," I offered, as I poked my head out the door. Nice thing about this place—the more crap you gave each other, the more you knew you were on the same page. The crap, I realized, was a more-than-welcome distraction on this particular day, when I wasn't sure how easy it was going to be to keep pushing the vortex out of my mind.

I sat down at my "desk of the day," which translated to "any spot that happens to be available," and fired up the computer that went with it. It was loading so slowly that I decided to head out to the nurse's desk.

Moving past the assignment board, I could see that the place was full, a rarity for 9 a.m. in the ER. "What the hell? Davidson die in the sleep room last night?" I asked.

Kath's response came quickly. "No he didn't, doughnut head. He busted his ass all night and he's grabbin' a quick shower before he signs off to you," she puffed.

"While we're waiting for Mr. Squeaky Clean, what's the rundown here?" I said.

"Six rooms full, plus a likely fracture in ortho, a laceration soaking in the procedure room, and a chest pain coming in by rig," she noted. "Davidson'll be here in about two minutes to sign off, so you have exactly 120 seconds to hike up your panties, put on your roller skates, and get ready."

I smiled. Gotta love that woman—a no-nonsense, strong-willed, five-foot-three-inch ball of fire—who made the perfect nurse. Unfortunately, her husband didn't have the balls to handle her strength and bolted—leaving her to deal with three teenage kids and a mortgage.

I was glad to have her on board, because it was going to be a busy day. That, however, wouldn't do much to change my approach to the situation. I might have slightly less time to talk with the patients, but they would still get my full attention, and, my usual shot at humor. They would also get explanations of their medical conditions devoid enough of doctor vernacular to actually be understandable.

Every patient that walks into an emergency room, or any clinic for that matter, deserves to feel that their healthcare professional is listening to them and cares about them as an individual. What we expect out of patients never ceases to amaze me. We put them into a cold room, make them take their clothes off, and then sit and wait for us to come in and start probing their bodily orifices. All of this after a perfunctory, five-second "Hello, I'm Dr. Krabb. Please bend over."

This, of course, is not a one-sided affair, and patients equally expect a lot from their doctors. I remain none too pleased with the lack of personal responsibility and the amount of noncompliance exhibited by so many of our patients. Nonetheless, it is not my job to treat them with any less respect or attention at a personal level. Every encounter sets the stage for a potential personal connection that can benefit the patient, no matter what the circumstance or complaint. And, I happen to believe that humor is the great equalizer when it comes to establishing that potential personal connection.

Bill Davidson was trudging down the hall, his scraggly wet mop of hair leaving a drip trail along the way. He resembled someone who had missed being run over by a car, but not by the semi truck behind it.

"Christ," I said. "You look like you were shot at and missed, but shit at and hit."

"I feel worse," he said. "The entire county, and their brothers, decided that last night was the night. For a little extra icing on the cake, they decided to drag with them their own virulent case of, I suspect, a norovirus, which has wasted no time setting up shop in my GI tract. So, dude, I'm out of here ASAP, after a brief sign out of what awaits you."

He did just that, and quickly disappeared into the morning sun. *Another one bites the dust, at least for a few days*, I thought.

I walked back over to the nurse's station and told Kath a joke—something to lighten up the mood before the craziness of the day began. We were both cackling when she suddenly stopped and announced, "Suit alert."

I kept on laughing until the moment of humor had passed, and turned my head to see Jim McQuinn walking down the hall toward us.

Jim and I were no strangers to each other, going back to the days when I did a blessedly short stint in a corporate-owned primary care clinic. I had come there from the private practice that I had joined right out of residency—a place where I might still be if our insurance reimbursements hadn't been so bad that we eventually had to close the doors, despite literally killing ourselves trying to keep the place open.

The last thing that I wanted to do at the time was join anything corporate. The other last thing that I wanted to do was leave the area, and thus my patients, many of whom were unable to follow me. Jim, a freshly-minted MBA, did my "welcome to the corporation" (euphemism for "let me show you who's in charge") interview. Given my responses to his questions, his pain in the fact that I had already been hired appeared to be difficult to conceal.

"Do you see yourself as a team player, doctor?"

"No, I don't," came my rapid reply.

The shock of anyone not answering the corporately rhetorical question in the affirmative apparently simultaneously tightened his brow and his anal sphincter. He managed to stammer out a question asking me to explain my heresy.

"If I wanted to spend my life being a team player, I wouldn't have gone to medical school," I explained. "Someone needs to be comfortable taking charge when your heart stops without feeling the need to form a committee and develop an action plan. If you would have asked me if I am comfortable working *with* a team, my answer would've been yes."

Over time our relationship didn't exactly blossom into a mutual admiration society. For some reason, he looked so much like he belonged in the office of the *Daily Planet* that I couldn't keep myself from calling him Jimmy, which he hated. I also was having a tough time grasping the corporate curriculum. It didn't take me long to realize that even as a "stakeholder" I couldn't seem to "align my incentives" and get on board with the "paradigm shift."

By that point Jim had slurped his way further up the ladder with the corporation and was feeling his oats when it came to exercising his newfound power. All of that slurping and a couple years of management experience had earned him a local magazine's "One of the 100 Most Influential People in Healthcare" award that year, which meant—without a doubt—that he was one of the one hundred most influential people in health care. And of course, influential in only the most noble of ways when it came to the health needs of patients.

The biggest issue the corporation had with its clinics, I later realized, was an internal structure that created a milieu in which no one in management was really held accountable for anything. No doubt this was because they had jumped so quickly into the "buy up every clinic in your area" mentality that had swept medicine at the time. Previously, they had owned a couple of hospitals and some outpatient surgery and physical therapy centers, and with these entities they did a stellar job. When they decided to jump into the clinic business, they were clearly not ready and started promoting lab assistants to office manager positions. It was the Peter Principle on steroids.

The biggest Peter of the bunch was Jim. Among a number of other asinine patient-nonfriendly initiatives, and a few truly dangerous ones, he was leading the charge toward centralized scheduling, whereby the corporation had total control over which doctor patients got to see, and when they got to see them. I fought him every step of the way. The central politburo, under this scheme, could theoretically maximize its resources by having all calls from patients trying to schedule an appointment directed into a single corporate office. Schedulers could then look to see which offices were less busy and attempt to direct patients their way—which wasn't always where the patient's own doctor may have been located.

This, of course, meant that patients who lived two blocks from the clinic they normally went to would sometimes get directed to another city to see a doctor, even though their own doctor, given the chance, would likely have squeezed them into their schedule the same day. With something like a sore throat, the biggest issue may have been logistics, but Mrs. Smith's acute shortness of breath and her complicated medical history were always most appropriately handled by the doctor who knew her best. Looking back, however, perhaps I was being too tough on the corporation. They did consistently refer to patients as *customers,* and I guess it's only fair that all *customers* got treated exactly the same way.

Treating them exactly the same way also meant that the corporation could look for new and exciting cost-saving measures *by doing everything exactly the same way.* What better way to promote this than to send a whole delegation of slurpers to the Far East to study how a major automobile manufacturer ran its assembly line? Jimmy and the rest of the group came back barely able to contain the excitement of passing on the knowledge gained during their "cost-saving" million-dollar Asian vacation to all of the providers in the clinics. I do love that insurance industry moniker—*provider.* Somehow, it always makes me think I'm part of the world's oldest profession.

In a nutshell, after being satiated with sushi and sake, their ultimate conclusion was that if all providers "on the line" each had their own wrench instead of having to walk extra steps to get one, the entire corporation would run much more efficiently. I concluded that if I were removing your gallbladder with a pair of pliers, I might be in agreement.

To the corporation, being outspoken at meetings was bad enough, but having the audacity to write about it in physician publications was tantamount to the most heinous of crimes. I had been writing for years as a physician advocate in various physician-oriented publications, and I saw no reason to begin to muffle my contempt for the changes that were happening in medicine. They saw it as a violation of their ownership of my time, my patients, my skills, and my soul.

In the midst of this debacle, I had an epiphany about how to respond to negative experiences in a positive way. I remember it vividly. It was 6 a.m., and I was driving home from an overnight moonlighting stint at a hospital in Saint Paul. I was reflecting on the crap I was dealing with and beating myself up for making a bad decision in joining the corporation. It wasn't anything earthshaking, just the sudden realization that a lot of bad experiences in life are simply learning experiences, and that treating them as such builds your character profile as an individual and strengthens your resolve to move forward.

I did move forward and used the experiences, and what I had already written, as a springboard to write a book about it. The book took a very blunt look at all of the "elephant in the room" issues in medicine that people weren't really talking about. No one was left without scrutiny, and that included doctors, patients, the insurance industry, the pharmaceutical industry, the legal industry, and your favorite congressman.

Part of my reason for eventually leaving primary care and going to emergency medicine was having a schedule that allowed me more time to further develop my creative side of music and writing. My book was one of a number of positive outcomes of that decision. It was also a great form of personal catharsis for me, since in it I could rant about everything that was going belly up in medicine and also add in anything I had previously written in other forums.

One of my favorite add-ins was a speech I gave the day I eventually left the corporation. I was the president of the medical school's alumni association at the time, which meant that I got to address the graduating class of medical students at Northrop Auditorium on the University of Minnesota campus. I shared the stage that day with an incredible African American physician, a man who would later run for president, and who, as a speaker, was quite a tough act to follow.

I think I did all right that day, speaking about our sacred oath and how being true to it had proven antithetical to grasping the curriculum of the corporation I had been working in. I recalled to them that my outspoken manner had gotten me called a number of names over the years, but the ones that I preferred to remember were "committed," "caring," and "forthright." I told them that undoubtedly along the way, someone who likely would never come in contact with "emesis"—and whose salary probably dwarfed theirs—would try to persuade them that "this is a new order" and that "physicians just don't want to give up control" and that "our first focus should be to satisfy our 'customers.'" Speaking truthfully, I noted that I personally was not anticorporate, antimanagement, or against any *ethical* means by which to deliver high-quality medical care at a reasonable cost. I closed by reminding them, however, that in any forum they chose to practice medicine, it was never okay to abandon the oath we all recited that day.

"I swear that man always picks the worst days to show up here," complained Kath, as I turned to face her.

"Trust me, his timing sucks," I said, as I recalled my further history with Jimmy.

Back at the ranch, it had become apparent that we weren't going to become congruent on the corporate curriculum, and both sides could see that this was a marriage made far south of heaven. I had even managed to piss off the PR department—how does *anyone* do that?

Here's how: I am in the clinic by myself—the only *provider* there the day that the PR department later decided was to be blown up into a shining example of a corporate clinic saving the world.

We were busy seeing patients when someone pushed through the front door, screaming that a car had just run off the busy road that went past the clinic. My nurse and I ran out to the scene, grabbing an automated external defibrillator as we went out the door. The police had just arrived on the scene and were pulling a middle-aged man out of the car through the driver's door.

We quickly assessed the guy, who had no pulse, and hooked up the AED. Two shocks later, the ambulance was loading him up for a ride to the hospital, pulse restored. We later heard that the man left the hospital, unscathed, three days later. *Cool*, I thought, and went back to work.

As they say, however, no good deed goes unpunished. The corporate PR machine was in no way going to let this incredible act of heroism, defined by us at the scene as just doing our job, go away without fanfare. They were speechless—a near physical impossibility amongst PR people—when I was reticent to comment about the event, and I gained yet another "friend" in the corporation.

There were enough irreconcilable differences, I finally concluded, to ask for a divorce before they concocted some duplicity on which to simply make me disappear. A friend in the group had tipped me off that the pot was already being stirred, and that Jimmy was the chief cook.

When we met to cement the details of the separation, Jimmy, his ever-smug self, blabbed out the artifice that "I should leave on good terms" because "you never know when we may meet again or have to work together again." I was more than pissed off with the upheaval he had created for my patients and with my life, and when we ran into each other in the hallway as I was leaving, I intimated, for his sake, that running into each other in an alley would not be the best place for our next "meeting." Reflecting on my conduct later I felt bad—sort of.

Turns out Jimmy was right—and wrong. We did meet again, and we worked in the same place, but not "together."

By that time I realized that I was not going to be able to continue in primary care, in any sort of iteration. When I started out in primary care, I got to do great things—like delivering babies, treating pneumonia, sewing up lacerations, and taking care of my patients in the hospital. As the power structure changed, instead of partnering with patients, I was expected to partner with the insurance industry, and to look at people as a set of numbers: A1C, LDL, BP, BMI—though I still got to treat your STD PDQ. While I always was, and still am, conscientious of the costs of services, I was suddenly expected to be the "steward of health care dollars"—meaning my job was to perfectly take care of you, the individual, while simultaneously saving the corporation gobs of money.

So, I went out and did some additional ER work and joined a consortium of ER docs who contracted with hospitals, including those of Jimmy's employer. Under this arrangement, we were employees, but not in the standard "under my thumb" sense of employment. Even though the hospital was owned by a corporation, as almost all now are, we weren't direct employees. Since we worked in the ER and dealt with emergencies, we also weren't open to the scheduling, testing restriction, and pay-for-performance manipulation of their other owned departments and clinics. Trying to deal with us, of course, drove now hospital-employed, corporate-mantra-spouting Jimmy crazy—especially when

I told him that the only pay-for-performance criterion that should be in place was the one where we correctly remove your gallbladder instead of your liver.

But alas, the insurance industry had the biggest pair of pliers, clamped squarely on the nuts of the hospital, which in turn clamped a slightly smaller pair on the nuts—or some other similarly sensitive body part—of every one of their directly employed physicians.

Pay for performance in primary care essentially meant figuring out a way to chain shut the refrigerator doors of your obese, hypertensive, diabetic, hypercholesterolemic, noncompliant patients, or end up getting paid the leftovers, from which had been removed the pay for performance "bonus." It meant being forced to try to make a decision between accepting the penalty for not using their recommended high percentage of generic drugs and accepting the penalty for exceeding their recommended low percentage use of brand-name drugs—all in order to get the numbers in line that made patients look good on paper. It also meant trying to coerce your patients to get the recommended checklist of screening tests or exams that weren't a bad idea, but also in many cases weren't something patients wanted—like chlamydia testing for your sixteen-year-old daughter. The ER, fortunately, was still almost completely exempt from this madness. Since "first do no harm" and ethics should still rule medicine, I matriculated to where I could exempt myself from avoiding them . . .

"Hiya, Jimmy," I chirped as I turned around and faced him. Startled at seeing me, he jumped back and walked around me. He ambled over to talk to the staff behind the nursing desk.

"Hello everyone," he began, "I hope you have a great day today."

"I'm sure we will," muttered Kath with minimal attempt to suppress a patronizing tone. "Why don't you stick around for a while and see what we do down here?" she asked.

"I'd *really* love to," he lied, "but I have four important meetings to go to today. I'm here to remind you, again, that lowering costs improves quality."

"Jimmy, did anyone ever tell you that all generalizations are bad?" I said, with a wink to Kath. She put her hand over her mouth in an unsuccessful attempt to suppress a laugh, while Jimmy looked at me quizzically. I added "ability to comprehend satire" to the growing list of attributes that weren't his strong suits.

"By the way, Jimmy," I said, "I gave your phone number to a patient the other day who wanted to make a comment about the signage in our rooms regarding antibiotics."

He looked excited. "You must mean our new posters that advertise the *Stop Antibiotic Over- Usage* campaign. We put a lot of time into that, to educate our patients to demand proper health care, backed by evidence-based medicine."

"I see," I nodded. "To have patients demand that we physicians stop guessing, and act as if we instead have had two and a half decades of education?"

The quizzical look returned.

"Just so you know," I said, "the patient I am referring to was excited also. I can't repeat his exact comments in mixed company, but he was definitely excited. He had called our new 'treatment over the phone' service. As it turned out, he had been improperly diagnosed with a condition for which he was then also prescribed a subtherapeutic dose of antibiotics—over the phone. He was just about ready to chalk it up to being his own mistake by the time he arrived here to have an actual person listen to his lungs. At that point, he spotted your poster on the exam room wall. Trust me, the irony of our phone treatment service in light of your antibiotic overusage campaign was not lost on him. I'm sure he'll be calling to "congratulate" you. If he doesn't, I'd suggest sending him a copy of our mission statement—you know, the one that says that we always put the *patient* first. Since it's in writing, and therefore not just patina, I'm sure he'll capitulate."

I walked to room three—first on the board—and picked up the chart, knocked, and entered the room. There sat a pleasant-looking woman who appeared to be in her mid-thirties, with a preschool male child seated next to her, and, per the chart, a twelve-year-old named Sam lying on his left side on the exam table. I extended my right hand to the woman.

"Hello, I'm Dr. Mann. Your name is?"

"Marie," she said.

"Nice to meet you, Marie." Looking at the small child seated next to her, I said, "Is this your driver?"

She laughed. "His name is Adam," she said.

I bent over toward the child. "Hello, Adam, give me five." I held out my open palm and Adam slapped it good and hard. "Did you bring your brother in to trade him for a new brother, or to get him fixed?" I asked.

"We need you to fix him because he has a tummy ache," Adam said.

I sat down at the computer desk in the room and punched in my username and password. I looked at Sam as his chart was loading on the computer and remarked: "Says here that you are a fan of sauerkraut pizza with chocolate chips, and ice cream with tomato sauce."

"Yuck!" Sam replied.

"Sorry," I said. "I use the same old jokes because I get a new audience in every room."

"How long has he been sick?" I asked Marie. She told me that he began complaining of nausea two days earlier. His appetite had also dropped off significantly yesterday, a sure sign of concern in any twelve-year-old. He had woken her up at 4 a.m. complaining of pain near his belly button, which now seemed to be worsening. He had not vomited, but she had noted a low-grade fever two hours earlier. *A pretty classic story for appendicitis*, I thought—so much so that any third-year med student should have come to the same conclusion.

"I looked up the symptoms on the Internet, and I'm worried about appendicitis," Marie said.

"You have to stop doing that or I'll be out of a job, Marie," I replied with a wink. "Let me look him over."

I had Sam sit up and checked his ears, nose, and throat and listened to his heart and lungs. I had him lay down on his back and gently palpated his upper abdomen, which was non-tender.

I began laying my hands on his lower abdomen, and as I did, I felt a strange sensation in my head that I could only describe as a feeling that my brain was literally expanding. The sensation was unnerving but not painful or uncomfortable, and what shocked me the most is that it didn't really feel all that unusual—like something I had experienced before, but couldn't quite put my finger on. I wanted nothing more right then than to sit down, put my head in my hands, and try to sort it out—kind of like the time I was working in the ICU trying to stabilize a rapidly decompensating patient, when word got to me that my college roommate had just been killed in a naval flight-training accident. Just as it was then, I had no choice but to push on with the task at hand.

Rather suddenly, I lifted my hands off of Sam's abdomen and backed up quickly.

"Are you okay?" asked Marie, obviously startled by my action.

"Yes . . . I am," I responded. "Just thinking . . . about something." I placed my hands back on Sam's abdomen and moved them toward the right lower quadrant. Normally I would at this point push gently on the abdomen and ask if the patient felt any pain. Instead, almost reflexively, I felt myself lift my hands off Sam's abdomen and back up, and I heard myself announce to Marie: "He has appendicitis."

She looked at me for what seemed like a very long few seconds, and said, "I trust you, Dr. Mann. But, can I ask, aren't there usually some tests to run?"

She was right. This was an instance where we usually would run some tests—some confirmatory, like a CAT scan, and some to help rule out other conditions, like a urinalysis and a complete blood count.

In the not so distant past, especially before CT was so readily available, surgeons chose to operate to remove a suspected inflamed appendix on the basis of the patient's history and their exam, with potentially some input from a couple of basic lab tests. In the pre "everyone gets a CT scan" days, removing an inflamed appendix 50 percent of the time was considered a pretty good surgical percentage. This of course meant that 50 percent of the time we also were opening up patients and removing a perfectly normal appendix—but we also weren't subjecting them to the cost and radiation of the scan (which, though it is very accurate in detecting a greater than six-millimeter appendix, is still not perfect). Some surgeons had also recently begun going back toward the original approach.

"Excuse me, Marie," I said, as I opened the exam room door. "I'm going to have the nurses call a surgeon so I can talk to him or her about Sam." I shuffled down the hallway toward the nurse's desk.

"You look a little green around the gills, Doc," Kath

said. "Davidson kiss you before he left?"

"The boy in room three has a nine-millimeter appendix," I heard myself say. "Can you put in a call to surgery, please?"

"Scuze me, Doc," she said. "You finally get one of those Star Trek handheld CT scanners you're always muttering about? How do you know he's got a nine-millimeter appendix?"

By then I was on my way to the ortho room. I took a deep breath, knocked, and opened the door. An eight-year-old was sitting on a man's lap, clutching his right wrist with his left hand. "How's it goin', guys?" I said.

"I don't want a shot," said the eight-year-old, whose chart noted his name was Reed.

"You won't need a shot," said his father, who told me his name was Mike.

I asked Mike, "Are we here to trade him in, or to fix him?"

Mike chuckled. "Some days . . ."

"Well," I said, "we can give you two four-year-olds or half a sixteen-year-old."

"I think we'll keep him," Mike said, "but we're worried about his right index finger. Got it caught in a car door today."

"Ouch," I said, as I reached to examine it. "We'll have to grab an X-ray and see if it is broken."

"Can't you tell that by feeling it?" Mike asked.

"Only if it's severely broken," I added.

As I gently began to feel the swollen finger, Mike persisted: "Tell me what you think."

"Transverse comminuted fracture of the middle phalanx with minimal displacement of the fragments," I heard myself say.

"That sounds bad," Mike observed.

"We'll see what the X-ray shows," I said as I left the room. I closed the door and leaned against the wall in the hallway, giving the "brain expansion" I'd experienced again while examining the finger some time to subside. This time the sensation didn't seem as unnerving as the first time—for which I was grateful. I was beginning to wonder if I should check myself in as a patient, but with our staffing at that moment, Dr. Mann would have to examine Dr. Mann. Besides, how the hell could I try to explain my vortex experience and what was happening that day to someone else when I was having a hard time quantifying it myself?

Pressing on, I pulled up Reed's chart on the hallway computer and entered the X-ray order. Kath was trucking down the hall. "Hoffman from surgery is on the phone. He's apt to hang up if you keep him waiting."

"I know all about Mr. 'Heal with Steel,' and I'm not impressed," I said. "No one else in the world ever has anything more important going on than what's happening in his world, even if he's sitting home picking his nose. The problem is—and he knows it—in this *system* his surgical group essentially has the hospital held captive."

"Whaddaya got?" Hoffman snarled as I picked up the phone.

"About thirty seconds," I said, "unless you want to interrupt your rounds and come down here to take care of the cardiac coming in by rig."

"Nurse says you think you have a kid with a nine-millimeter appendix, but I don't see a CT scan result anywhere in his chart."

"Need you in the cardiac room now, Doc—rig's here," boomed Kath, loud enough to be heard on both ends of the phone.

"Didn't get one yet, but you can see him down here in room three—gotta go," I said and hung up the phone.

I ran down the hall behind her. The ambulance crew was in the process of transferring a frail-looking woman named Maude onto our gurney, plugging her oxygen line into our wall source, and hanging her IV bag onto one of our IV poles. Kath was hooking her up to do an EKG. Maude looked right into my eyes: "We've met before," she said.

"And you're still alive?" I winked.

"Last time I was here, you said I was held together with glue, tape, and twine, but you fixed me up real well."

"You forgot to mention wire, but otherwise you are pretty much correct. What's wrong, Maude?"

"I woke up at about 2 a.m. with this heaviness in my chest. So, I got up and drank some Maalox. You know, Doc, ever since Bill died I've had this heartburn problem, and when the girls and I get together and play cards and have a cocktail—well, when we go to Rose's house, and you know she buys that cheap chip dip, and she starts rambling on about . . ."

"Maude," I interrupted, "I hate to cut you off, but are you having any pain in your chest right now?" I said, as I laid my hand on her sternum.

"Well, it's kind of a heaviness . . ." Kath was ready to run the EKG and had motioned to Maude to stay still and quiet as she hit the start button.

"Call a code sixty-eight, stat," I said to the nurse behind me.

"That's the code to ready the cardiac catheterization lab," Kath said, "and you haven't even . . . seen . . . the . . . EKG . . . yet . . ." she stammered in a sentence that slowed as it finished, while she handed me an EKG that we both clearly recognized had massive ST segment elevations across the lateral precordial leads.

"I'll call the code," said the nurse, as she took off toward the desk.

Kath turned her head and stared at me with a look that was equal parts bewilderment and shock. "What the hell is going on with you?" she demanded.

"I really don't know," I said as I left the room.

I moved on to room three to find a deep finger laceration, sustained as a work-related injury by contact with a sharp piece of metal. The nurse asked me if I needed any extra instruments to help further explore the wound to rule out any deeper tendon injury. I felt the wound, said no, and quickly repaired it. When I smiled and asked her if she could be pregnant and about the need for any pain medication, I got a wink and heard a pleasant sixty-eight-year-old voice say: “Not this week, and I think I’ll do okay with Tylenol, doctor.”

“You know,” I said, “we could petition your work to cover a two-week recuperation period in the Bahamas, but you’d have to take your doctor with.”

“I’d have to okay it with my husband first,” she said.

“There’s always a complication,” I laughed as I left the room.

Chapter 6

The day moved along as I shuffled over to room two, opened the door, and looked inside. It seemed like almost a full minute that I stood in the doorway laughing—partly because of the relief it gave me, and more so because I don't think anyone could resist the hilarity of a four-month-old boy wearing a bib that announced: "Lock up Your Daughters."

I treated his ear infection, and as I stepped out of the room, one of the nurses directed me to the critical care room that had been earlier occupied by Maude, who by this time was getting her coronary arteries squirted.

There sat a forty-two-year-old male with his head in his hands. As I entered the room, he looked up at me, and it was obvious that he was quite uncomfortable. The note on the one-page paper chart on the door had announced: "Sudden onset of the worst headache he has ever had."

I talked with him briefly as I placed my hands on his neck and then ran them alongside his skull up to his forehead. Kath came into the room shortly after I hit the call button, and I asked her to reach Dr. Kirk Lisne for me ASAP.

"You mean the neurosurgeon?" she said.

"That's him," I answered.

"Didn't you two go to medical school together?" she said.

"Indeed we did," I replied.

We left the room, and I grabbed a quick cup of coffee, knowing that unless Kirk was in surgery, he would be on the phone momentarily. When the ER called a neurosurgeon directly, they knew we needed them quickly.

Kirk was quite a guy, and a helluva surgeon. In our early years of medical school, I don't think anyone suspected that he would end up in a neurosurgery residency. It wasn't until years later in our training that we realized that the correlation between crazy behavior early in medical school and the later acceptance of incredibly demanding medical residencies was a direct one.

Kirk's best-remembered behavior from those early days was an alternate personality named "Dickie," who had a propensity to get up and dance atop anything he could stand on at parties—not altogether a bad beginning for a guy who would eventually be in charge of operating on your brain.

I laughed when I thought of similarly interesting behaviors that, as students, we observed amongst the seasoned physicians we interacted with. Cam Peters, a local pathologist who taught at the med school, had belonged to a national medical fraternity when he was in med school, and the frat was in the process of rebuilding itself. Cam decided that our school needed to open up a new chapter of the fraternity, and several of us were more than eager to get on board. I, in particular, was excited, because when I was in college Saint John's didn't have any fraternities, and I'd always wanted to belong to one. I really wanted to see how these groups operated, and as such, I put in a lot of time to get the local group up and running. Either because of this, or because they were scraping the bottom of the barrel, I was elected a chapter officer and eventually a national officer.

This meant I got to attend national meetings—sometimes in interesting places, and sometimes in Detroit. The meetings themselves, pretty much comprised of men, were somewhat boring, but afterward all hell would break loose. It became quickly obvious to me that the combination of alcohol, and the release from the constraints of their practices, turned these pillars of their communities into blithering high school sophomores—which meant that as students, we had a helluva good time.

I'm not sure which medical school honed these guys' abilities in pyrotechnics, but lighting off fireworks under police cars and being able to escape without detection is not a skill for the lighthearted. Neither is being able to jump unharmed into the swimming pool from the second story balcony of a frat house. Fortunately, the closest I ever came to being scathed was being called out for not wearing my dinner jacket as I crossed the lobby of the Augusta Country Club. Guess I won't get invited for membership—oh, well.

"Dr. Mann, Dr. Lisne is on the phone," rang out Kath's voice. I walked to the desk and she handed me the phone.

"Derek, how are you?" came the voice from the other end.

"Doing well, thank you, Kirk. How are you and Julia?"

"Feisty as ever," he replied. "What can I do for you?"

"I've got a forty-two-year-old guy here who I think has

a leaking berry aneurysm in the Circle of Willis. As you are well aware, we don't do neurosurgery here, and I'd like to get this guy to your facility ASAP."

"Happy to help," came the reply. "Obviously, send him by ambulance, and have your radiologist forward me a copy of the MRI."

The short silence that followed seemed like an eternity before he said, "You still there, Derek? Anything wrong?"

"I want to send him right over, Kirk, because I think he needs your attention immediately. I didn't want to risk wasting even a minute of time getting the study done here, so I don't have an MRI."

There was another short silence, followed by: "I know you, Derek, so I'll trust you and pull some strings and have stat MRI waiting for him on arrival."

"Thanks, Kirk," I said, and hung up the phone.

Kath, standing behind me, was still giving me the confused look when she said, "X-ray results are back in ortho, and I'm tagging along on this one."

I knew it was useless to argue, so we walked to the ortho room, and I logged into the computer and pulled up Reed's results. Kath and Reed's father, Mike, looked over my shoulder at the radiologist's reading of Reed's X-ray: "Transverse comminuted fracture of the middle phalanx with minimal displacement of the fragments."

"That sounds word-for-word like what you said after you felt his finger," said Mike. "I thought you said you couldn't tell me what was going on without the X-ray."

Kath intervened. "Dr. Mann was right when he said that," she stated. She shot me a look: "He's having some sort of *exceptional* day today."

You don't know the half of it, I thought.

Working in silence, we put a splint on the finger and referred him to ortho.

By then, Dick Johnson had arrived, so we had two MDs staffing until the end of the shift. Dick was a few years older, but hadn't lost a step. He could really kick ass when it came to getting the job done when it was necessary, and on this day, it was necessary.

We'd worked another couple of hours when Kath motioned me over to the nurse's desk. "Sam's in surgery," she said. "His CT report is in the chart."

I pulled up the report: "Abdominal organs are well-visualized and within normal limits. Bowel appears normal with no signs of obstruction. Appendix is enlarged at approximately 9mm. Findings consistent with acute appendicitis."

What the hell? I thought. *Now I'm predicting X-ray* and *CT scan results?* There was no doubt in my mind that at any second, my alarm clock would go off and end this weird dream. No such luck. I went back to work and waited for the next brain expansion—which never came.

We were running our butts off to try to keep up—semi-successfully. Like most days in the ER, the majority of our patients appreciated that effort. They still didn't like the wait times, but they knew we were doing our absolute best. People, however, are never at their best when they are sick, in pain, or dealing with a family member with a medical emergency. I understand that, which is why I try to be understanding and to cut them slack whenever I can. I also realize that they are doing the same with us when it's extremely busy, though we as the staff have no control over chaos in the outside world that drives unpredictability—and today I'd had enough internal unpredictability of my own.

There are times, however, when anyone's patience gets tried and a bit of education seems appropriate—like the case of the well-dressed gentleman who was livid about the whopping twenty-four minutes he spent waiting for me to check his sore throat that had started that very morning. I had just spent the last several minutes trying to gently break the news to a patient that the spots that I saw on his chest X-ray could well be cancer. Mr. $300 Italian Shoes made no bones about sharing his opinion that if he had to wait this long to have his throat examined, we here in the ER knew nothing about staffing and customer service.

We finished up the visit.

"What do you do for a living, sir?" I asked.

"I own a car dealership," came the reply.

"Well then," I said, "given your experience with customer service, I'll pass on your concerns to hospital administration. We'll see if they are willing to keep ten doctors here in the ER at all times so the next time you come in, you won't have to wait more than one or two minutes to have your sore throat checked."

I looked at his shoes. "Given the extra staffing, I suspect you won't mind paying $1,000 for the privilege."

"A thousand dollars to get my throat looked at?" he huffed as he left the room.

Fortunately, patients like that, and doctors who don't care, are relative rarities. I told Dick Johnson about the exchange. He laughed and noted that in a situation like that, his usual response was: "And what time was your appointment, sir?"

Of course we all know—because even doctors are patients—that an appointment *anywhere* doesn't guarantee punctuality on either side of the desk, but medical clinics are probably the worst.

Sometimes it is the fault of doctors, who either overbook, underplan, are slow, or simply aren't very good at multitasking—which, unless you are a dermatologist, is an absolute necessity. In my private practice, by most accounts, we did overbook, which was also an absolute necessity if we were going to keep the doors open with the reimbursements we were being offered.

Sometimes it is the fault of patients, whose expectations at a single office visit of fifteen minutes are staggering. Part of this is our own fault as primary care physicians, when we tell patients to make a list of their issues and bring it to the visit—though there should be some common sense involved in what people expect to get accomplished in that amount of time. Kind of like taking your car in for an oil change, and after you drop it off, you say: "Oh, by the way, rebuild the engine while it's here. I'll pick it up in an hour. This is all covered by the co-pay for the oil change, right?"

Really, this is all part of the territory, and both sides need to be respectful of the needs and the realities of the other party. There are times in medicine, however, when you have no choice but to just do what needs to be done—schedules be damned.

I said to Dick, "Did I ever tell you about the 'toe incident' when I was in private practice?"

"The toe incident?"

"Well, that's how I refer to it when I tell the story."

I proceeded to tell Dick about a typical extremely busy day in our primary care clinic, when, in the midafternoon, I moved onto the next patient to be seen and picked up the chart from its holder on the wall next to the exam room door. I looked at the chief complaint, which read: "Needs antibiotics."

Inwardly I thought: *Simple enough—might allow me to get somewhat back on schedule.* I knocked, opened the door, and went in. Seated on the exam room table was a well-dressed young man in his mid-twenties who appeared to be in no distress. I introduced myself, made some small talk, and then asked what I could do for him.

"I need some antibiotics," he said.

"Why's that?" I replied.

"I cut my toe off," he said.

"Ouch!" I replied. "How did that happen?"

"I cut my toe off," he said again.

"Did . . . you . . . have an accident?" I said.

"No," he said, "I'm a cutter and I needed to cut my toe off, so I did."

I took a deep breath and looked at him. "How are you doing now?" I said.

"I'm doing great," he replied. "I just need some antibiotics because I'm afraid that I could get an infection."

He took off his shoe and sock. I observed a toe, amputated down to the first phalanx, with a flap of skin neatly sewn over the end with what appeared to be fishing line.

We talked some more, and I further discovered that he was, by all appearances, completely calm and coherent. I told him I thought we could help him, but I needed to make a couple of phone calls. I left the room and asked my nurse to put a call in to psychiatry, while I called a surgeon friend of mine—one whose humanity was fortunately not beaten out of him or surgically removed during his residency.

I described the situation to him, to which he replied: "Wow, that's incredible. From the way you describe it though, Derek, I can't really do much more for him, other than offer him a job if he's looking for work."

"Thanks, Bob," I said. "I appreciate your help."

By then psychiatry was on the phone, and after discussing the situation in detail, they set him up for a stat outpatient follow-up and a list of emergency resources to use as necessary.

I went back to the room and he pleasantly accepted everything I gave him, including a prescription for Keflex.

I asked him to come back to see me in a week to make sure that everything was healing okay, and that there weren't any complications. Despite how smoothly the appointment had gone, in the back of my mind I really didn't expect to see him again. Other than the need to see me for antibiotics, he was obviously a do-it-yourselfer.

Surprisingly to me, however, he was back on my schedule in exactly one week. I stepped in to see him and he greeted me with a pleasant hello. He told me things were going well, and removed his shoe and sock, and indeed the wound was healing well. Before he left, he told me he would continue to follow up with psychiatry even though he really didn't think he needed it. The whole appointment took about five minutes, as compared to the nearly one hour that was necessary for me to spend with him the week before.

As he left, he showed me his key ring, and on it were the two bones from his amputated toe, boiled clean, drilled, and held in place with a metal ring.

"Did you ever see him again?" asked Dick.

"No I didn't," I said. "Too bad, because I really liked him."

We moved on and continued to treat the masses, including those afflicted with the virus Bill Davidson had warned us about.

Several patients later I picked up a chart with the noted chief complaint of "rectal problem," and chastised myself as I realized that my brain had decided to route into a familiar pathway in thinking that this was probably another case of "Davidson's Disease."

As a physician, one of the worst things you can do is to go into any patient encounter with preconceived notions. This especially includes patients dubbed "frequent flyers." It is extremely easy to get led down the primrose path by a preconceived notion or a previous bit of history, and in the medical world, correcting a wrong turn isn't as easy as just putting the car into reverse. Here, at least initially, the boy who cried wolf has to be assumed credible.

Stepping into the room, I introduced myself to the patient and asked him what the problem was.

"My ass hurts," came the reply. Not an easy situation in which to infuse humor to ease the patient, I was thinking, but as it turned out, I wasn't the one who needed to take the lead. Sometimes patients themselves open up the dialogue, and it becomes apparent quite quickly that we both can converse at a very base, and humorous, level.

As he gave me his history, I suspected he was dealing with a thrombosed external hemorrhoid, a hemorrhoid that had literally bled into itself and caused a painful clotted mass. I explained to him what I suspected he had, and told him that if this was the case, we would need to spread his cheeks, inject some Novocain, and make an incision to expel the clot.

He looked at me and asked, "Are you going to lower the lights and light some candles first?"

"Only if we smoke a cigarette together afterwards," I replied.

The banter continued, and by the time the nurse and I had him in position to make the incision, we were all laughing to the point where I had to stop for a minute.

"You realize how crazy this is?" I said to the patient. "I am about to take a scalpel to your ass, and all three of us are laughing about it."

"Press on, Doc," came the reply. "You're doing great."

Later in the afternoon I went into a room and was greeted by a smiling elderly woman. "You look like a pleasant young man," she said.

"I only bite on Wednesdays, and today is Tuesday so you are in luck," I replied.

"I like you already," she said, "which is good, because I think I need a new doctor."

"Why's that?" I asked.

"Because my current doctor refuses to refill my blood pressure medications unless I have a breast exam."

Fuming underneath in sympathy for her, I said: "I don't think your doctor is likely being inappropriate, if that's what you were worried about."

"Of course she's not," she answered, "unless she has a thing for seventy-four-year-old breasts. I know that's not the issue," she continued, "and I know about how you doctors get pressured to push patients into doing certain things. I just wish someone would listen to me and let me do what *I* want, and nothing more. I'm not going to take some fancy cholesterol pill no matter what my cholesterol number is, and no one is going to make me let them put a three-foot rubber hose up my behind. I feel like they look at me like a set of *numbers* that they have to get just right, and not as a person who didn't get to age seventy-four by being a pushover."

"But you are interested in your blood pressure number," I said.

"Yes, and that's it," she said. "I know there are some other tests and things that aren't bad things to do, but I just don't want them, and that's what I told my doctor—several times."

I told her I would be happy to refill her blood pressure pills for a month, and that I would also be happy to be her doctor, except that I only work here in the emergency department, which means we would have to help her find someone else in primary care that she could see on a regular basis.

"That's fine," she said, "but just don't send me to someone that looks young enough to be my great-grandson, and who doesn't have enough experience to find his ass with both hands and a road map."

I looked at her and we both burst out laughing.

"It's really too bad that I don't work in the clinic," I told her, "because I'd love to have you as a patient. You know, though," I said, "as doctors it seems that we have a very short window between when we all look young enough to be wet behind the ears and old enough to be senile."

"About two years or so—so I better let you get back to work, because you are running out of time," she said with a wink.

Walking back down the hall, I noticed Kath was coming toward me.

"Dr. Lisne just called and said to tell you that the MRI was done and that they were going in to clip a berry aneurysm and would you meet him for lunch someday to help him pick some stocks? Does that make any sense to you?"

"Yes, and yes, and I don't know what the hell is going on," I said as I walked back into our changing room. In the space of twenty-four hours, I'd had some sort of incredible mind-expanding experience while sitting in a tree, and then had just worked an ER shift where shit happened to me that I couldn't begin to explain.

Fortunately, my shift of seeing patients was over, but unfortunately, the "paperwork" had just begun. If nothing else, though, I thought it might help to block the confusion clouding my mind in the wake of the strange day I'd just had.

We still referred to it as paperwork, even though it was now all done on an electronic medical record, or EMR. I had a couple of hours of charting to do so that the hospital could get paid, so that I had a good medico-legal record of today's patient visits, and most importantly, so that there was an accurate, detailed, and understandable summation of what had transpired during the visits for use by future clinicians. The last part of that equation had more recently come under siege as clinicians had begun to succumb to cookie-cutter, cut-and-paste versions of visit notes that somehow satisfied the reimbursement part of the equation, but many times were practically useless from a clinical standpoint.

I stuck with the dictated version of note making, which satisfied me that I was leaving behind a reasonable record, while I simultaneously tried to suppress my tendency toward verbosity and the risk of a chart coming back to me with the words: "Bullshit, Bullshit, Bullshit" stamped on it.

When I finally finished all of the dictation, I realized that Dick Johnson would be done with his shift soon and the new crew would be taking over. I decided to look over and sign off some of my previously dictated chart notes to waste a little time until he was done so we could talk a bit. Conversations with Dick were always rousing and political.

For those of us who were still dictating notes, the medical records department took the digital files of our dictations and ran them through voice recognition software, and left them for us to sign off. This, of course, was not error-proof, though the technology involved had improved at a rapid rate. Because of this, it was important to read these dictations and correct them before signing off on them, though not everyone did.

Some of the errors in voice recognition dictation were simple punctuation issues. Some were incorrect (like skipping the word "not"). Some were downright hilarious, though not *necessarily* incorrect, like the one I ran across regarding birth control use which obviously substituted another word that sounded like "late," as it stated: "She says she hasn't been laid on the Depo-Provera so she doesn't think she could be pregnant . . ."

Dick Johnson walked in, grabbed a cup of coffee, and sat down.

"Ah, bonding with your EMR," he winked. "They say it's not about the quantity—it's about the quality time you spend with those you love."

"Well, there's plenty of quantity here, which bears no direct relation to quality, unless you consider quality to be directly related to the amount of peripheral data we are now compelled to collect for our payors," I muttered.

"Gee," he said sarcastically, "I thought the whole concept of an EMR was to improve the quality of patient care."

"In the apocryphal sense, of course it is," I replied in kind. "Just like the sun always shines in Seattle, the Supreme Court has ruled that the insurance industry is not allowed to practice medicine, and government shouldn't be allowed to either."

"So, what is allowed in through the front door is not the same as what comes in through the back door?"

"Precisely. Government won't tell us how to practice medicine. If, however, its EMR data says you used your medical judgment and bankrupted the entire medical complex by giving someone an antibiotic for bronchitis, they'll find a way to decrease what they pay you, based on their definition of 'value.' Obviously, we are all worried about overuse of antibiotics, but that kind of interference also smells like a method of restricting patients from accessing the system."

Dick handed me a cup of coffee.

"I haven't seen you in a while, and we've been so busy I haven't even gotten the chance to ask you how you've been," I said.

"Pretty well," he replied. "Just fighting the usual battles."

"Life or medicine?" I asked.

"Yes," he answered.

Dick was a guy who, like me, didn't do well with the concept of "going along to get along" when it came to the changes he saw in medicine, or with whatever new scheme the medical establishment had cooked up.

I added some hazelnut creamer to my coffee and took a sip. As much as I wanted to spill my guts to him about what had happened to me during my eight hour shift, I couldn't. He'd probably run a drug test on me. I decided to go along with the conversation.

"I think I have finally figured out what frustrates me the most these days about being a doctor," Dick mused.

"Thought you knew that long ago," I offered.

"Probably did," he answered, "but I needed to put it in the form of a decent metaphor. What really frustrates me, and what I somehow need to learn to deal with, is the propaganda arm of the insurance industry, which has gotten quite adept at diverting attention away from the real issues in order to cement the need for their high-buck health plans."

He continued: "I didn't go into medicine expecting to

get my ass kissed. I also didn't expect to have a well-oiled propaganda machine set itself up as the benevolent friend of the patient, while trying to blame physicians for the lack of 'quality' in health care as it applies to overall clinical outcomes. You faced it already in primary care, and I know it's on its way to the ER. Give me decent metal, metal that I can work with, and I'll build you a decent car. Send me rusty metal that has no intention of holding its shape, and you'll get a crappy car, no matter how much 'quality' I put in my work. Of course, it's much smoother for your insurance company and your congressman's re-election to blame me for the bad outcome than it is to blame the rusty metal."

He took a sip of coffee and added, "As physicians, we spend a huge amount of time caring for a subset of our population that is the most obese, noncompliant, crappy-lifestyle set of people in the world. Despite this, the *machine* has spent millions to hammer home the concept that it is our responsibility *alone* as physicians when what rolls off the line is an Edsel instead of a Mercedes. It's a win-win for them. If patients get better, they win. If they don't, there's always pay for performance, and they win. Fortunately, not everyone we take care of behaves poorly, but their numbers are *growing*—pardon the pun. Something like 5 percent of the population consumes about 50 percent of what we spend on health care, so we are dealing with some pretty rusty vehicles."

"So, why are you still building cars?" I asked.

"Same reason you are—because we care about the cars. By the way, I'm not a raging anti-insurance industry guy.

We need the insurance industry, but we also need it, and the federal government, to have way less influence on how medicine is practiced. Is our federal government really efficient at running *anything*, anyway?

"Usually, the value of a product is decided by those who are buying it and those who are producing it. Where else but now in medicine do you give the government and the insurance industry your money, and let them decide where the value is in the product you access? Or worse, decide if you get to access it at all? When we stop their meddling, and patients have more skin in the game, we can sit in an exam room with a patient and make decent medical decisions *together*, instead of fending off Hobson's choice. As docs, we could also get rid of their feedback flack when we appropriately say no."

"How's that?" I asked.

He proceeded to tell me about the last patient on his shift, whose chief complaint was anxiety.

"A reasonable enough complaint to bring into the emergency room, depending on the circumstance," he said. In this particular casc, however, when he had asked her why she was anxious, her response was: "Planning a vacation is *so* stressful."

"As she was telling me this, I looked at her chart and noticed that she was already on four different psychotropic medications. It wasn't long before she informed me that the reason for her visit was to procure more Xanax, so I excused myself and pulled up her profile on the state pharmacy databank. Lo and behold, she had gotten three prescriptions for Xanax in the last fifteen days from three different clinics."

"You're shocked that someone came into the ER and tried to ding you for a controlled substance prescription?" I inquired.

"Like you and I both don't know that that happens multiple times a day," came the reply. "Did you hear me say why it was that she was so anxious—*planning a vacation is so stressful.* I'm not shocked that she came here looking for Xanax, but apparently people don't think they need to even bother anymore with some story like 'my father is going through another sex change operation and I just can't handle it.'

"The medical complex is just as much at fault for this as the patients," he continued. "The way psychiatry is practiced, by some physicians, seems to have gotten completely out of hand. I know about the time constraints that you have mentioned that primary care physicians are under, and I assume psychiatrists face the same issues, including the fact that getting people in to decent counselors is never a foregone conclusion. I realize the tremendous pressure and lack of resources these guys deal with in treating these patients. However—does anyone ever try anymore to wean people back off of these medications, or do they just continue them and add another drug?"

"Seems to me to be more of the latter," I observed.

"Pure and simple case of DOD," Dick muttered.

"DOD?"

"Yes, DOD—my newest aphorism, proposed as an addition to the DSM—which is of course the Diagnostic and Statistical Manual of mental disorders as published by the American Psychiatric Association. You obviously know about the DSM—which, in my estimation—leaves one person in northern Utah, a little old lady in the south of France, and two hermits in northern Mongolia as the only four people left in the world who can be classified as mentally 'normal.' DOD stands for *diagnosis obsession disorder*, and I see no reason why the DSM should not let me include it in their next update, because the whole damn thing is a testament to diagnosis obsession."

"Aww, you're just upset because you know that somewhere in that manual there is a diagnosis that fits you perfectly," I said, simultaneously wondering if my last two days weren't an indication that my own form of psychosis was forthcoming.

Dick laughed. "Listen, Mann—you know damn well that both of us fit a diagnosis in there somewhere or neither one of us would be working here. The way I see you run around, I'm surprised that your breakfast meal every day growing up wasn't Ritalin and cornflakes."

"Barely escaped that, and lucky for me. I always figured that if they force-fed me medications for ADHD, all that would be left would be a pile of dust. I had a girlfriend once that told me that I only had one speed—faster."

"Depending on what you are referring to," Dick interjected, "that's not necessarily the type of information you want floating around the dating circuit."

"Duly noted," I nodded. "I do know what you mean about the DSM, though. Mr. Reitman in high school science always referred to the world as being comprised of two types of people—the lumpers, and the splitters. I figured out soon enough that I was a lumper."

"How's that?"

"Just a difference in worldview, with both groups being necessary to the advancement of knowledge and society. Lumpers stand back, observe the big picture, and from that observation try to bring clarity to the picture by coalescing parts of it into meaningful units that can interact more precisely. Splitters, on the other hand, look at just about anything and decide that the world is better served by further separation or categorization."

"So, nuclear physicists would be—pardon the pun—the ultimate splitters."

"Indeed they would," I said. "Obviously at that level, the splitters win out, and much of our endeavor for knowledge appropriately involves splitting. However, there comes a point where splitting that seems to be done for the sake of splitting begins to become counterproductive—kind of like serving a single apple pie to a regiment of soldiers by cutting the slices one-sixteenth-inch thick. That, to me, is the DSM."

Dick laughed.

"Lumpers don't always get it right either," I added. "Since this country is always in flux and operates like a big ongoing social experiment, some things just can't be that black and white, but some can. In my perfect world, we would agree to satisfy vague legalities so we could continue to build playground equipment for kids, and if necessary post danger signs on them in multiple languages, including Swahili, that exempt their makers from liability. That kind of common sense could be applied to medical tort reform as well."

"I'm all for that," Dick said.

"My concern," I concluded, "is that in our zest for knowledge and the improvement of society, the lumpers don't speak up and we lose the big-picture view of what is really going on. It's kind of like running full speed into a forest without looking around or stopping to catch your breath and take an assessment of where you are. Pretty soon you're just plain lost; the whole scene is just too big to wrap your arms around—kind of like big government and big medicine. This is why, at least in one area of medicine, we've learned to take a 'pause for the cause.' In highly charged circumstances such as surgeries and during code blue cardiac arrests—as you know—we review where we are, so we don't lose sight of the big picture or cut off the wrong toe. From a societal standpoint, I think we also need to take a pause for the cause with a number of issues that we have already made great strides with, and step back and take a look at the big picture with a common-sense attitude—and also avoid cutting off the wrong toe."

"I agree completely," Dick said. "However, common

sense and political capital make strange bedfellows. Hence, my three-point plan to save America."

"And that is?"

"Term limits, a balanced budget amendment, and a flat tax."

"You are going to get congressmen to vote themselves out of a job?"

"Why not? The fox can't guard the henhouse forever."

"You should just hang up the stethoscope and run for office, Dick."

"Not the worst idea ever," he said as he got up, refilled his coffee cup, and said hello to Mark Lansing, who was just walking in to pick up his mail.

"Problem is," Dick continued, "I'm afraid that my brand of common sense may not play well in Poughkeepsie, or anywhere else these days, for that matter. The world is becoming convinced that if we just *educate* people enough, they will then behave perfectly and all of our problems will be solved. Using medicine as an example, you and I both know that unless you've been buried underground for the last thirty years, you are well aware of the dangers of alcohol, drugs, smoking, and obesity. At a certain point, your fate needs to lie in your own hands. Blaming lack of education for our problems just ends up taking the onus off of individuals and putting it on broader society—which, by itself, cannot exert the type of control necessary to deal with the issues we now face. The fact is, society has begun to realize that it can't buy its way out of this mess—and now *has* started to try to exert control. The irony is, people who want to have their burger their way and then demand that society pick up the tab may end up not getting a burger at all."

He cleared his throat. "Further *educating* the populace may make certain politicians and a few other people sleep better at night because they think that they are doing something, but what they are doing more than anything is just patting themselves on the back. I'm not against education. I'm against using the 'lack' of it as an excuse for bad behavior. Remember the canard that all of that preventative medicine we paid for a few years back was supposed to fix the high cost of medical care?"

"Indeed I do," I replied.

"Well, obviously it didn't. But apparently, we now have a real solution. A medical student who just rotated through here told me that they are now being educated to be *stewards* of the health care dollar. If I, as a patient, am not scared as hell about having cost be the *first* thing your doctor thinks about when she walks into the exam room, I should be. I should be equally scared if the practice of medicine is getting so screwed up that the best and brightest individuals no longer want to join its ranks, and instead head toward business or engineering, where they also expect to make better money.

"Anyway," he said, "now that I'm done rambling on, what's *your* plan to save medicine?"

The rapid-fire banter with Dick, I realized, was in its own strange way giving my mind a rest from overprocessing the events of the day, so I indulged him.

"I gave you a copy of my book for Christmas last year," I said. "Didn't you read it?"

"Parts of it, but give me the short synopsis."

"I'll try to do that, but it may come off like another sound bite—so you need to read the whole book, where I do summarize what we need to do.

"The overall message is that we need to give control of medical decisions back to patients and doctors, and deflate the insurance and political football that health care has become. As this plays out, some consumers of health care will love it, and some will hate it, because in *my* system, everyone pays something to access health care—even if it starts out as a dollar on a sliding-scale fee system. As individuals further realize that 'insurance' is not prepaid health care and opt for better choices, the 'first dollar' coverage concept that created this mess will become a complete historical anecdote. Prepaid health care policies are no more justifiable than auto insurance policies that would try to cover gasoline, tires, and car washes, anyway.

"In the end, when such policies are gone, we can separate appropriate payment for health *care* from the forced payment for health *maintenance* of individuals who refuse to live healthy lifestyles. Then, *most* people will be allowed to pay for what they really need, and they will be able afford decent health care."

"That wasn't very short," laughed Dick.

"Best I could do without spouting just another sound bite," I answered. "I've said it before, and I'll say it again: I simply don't know how we as a country can sleep at night, spending medical dollars on the things we do, while knowing that we are not first meeting at least the basic medical needs of all of our children—not to mention things like childhood diabetes and leukemia, which have nothing to do with lifestyle."

"So," Dick inquired, "when are *you* running for office?"

"My friend Gus recently said that you probably won't qualify to run for office if you think before you open your mouth. I'm not sure that that always applies to me, but either way the answer is—the day after my first real UFO sighting."

Chapter 7

I don't favor the connotation that comes along with the statement "I really need a beer." In this case, however, I really needed a beer. The good news was that there was no better guy to have a beer with than Mark Lansing. Mark was working three different jobs now, after having started in the ER at about the same time I did. He was always ready to take the next challenge, and he had branched out to do some work in information technology, as well as in a cutting-edge endocrine clinic. That meant that he was spending less time working with us, and I didn't get to see him as often. He was also putting two kids through college, soon to add a third. When I asked him how long he thought he could keep up this pace, he told me he already had his retirement plan figured out. "What's that?" I asked. He replied that he had already inquired of his children which one of them would hire him as his or her pool boy.

Despite his incredibly busy schedule, Mark was always at the ready when beer was on the line. He was also an accomplished guitarist, despite his insistence to the contrary. For years we had had a running date at the annual Nobel Conference at Gustavus Adolphus College in Saint Peter, where we would show up, hang around campus, and pretend that the years hadn't passed. Afterward we would hang out, do a little amateur astronomy, partake of the goodness of the fermented grain, and jam out on our guitars.

As we walked across the street to the local Legion club, I noticed the sign announcing the Bird Dogs band. "I know these guys," I said, "and this should be fun."

I had decided that my vacation restarted the next day, and my involvement with the vortex could wait until then. Wrong again . . .

We walked in and the place was packed. There was a heavy din of conversation, and the air hung heavy with odors of beer and pizza. Just our kind of place.

The band was on break, and we grabbed the one open table left in the place, along the far wall close to the band. Piped through the overhead speakers, a song was being sung by an actor who had recently decided that his on-screen fame somehow gave him license to further expand his creative horizons. I shook my head as I muttered his name.

"I didn't know he could sing," observed Mark.

I stared at him as I tugged my ear.

"I didn't know he was trying to sing," added Mark.

"If Madonna writes a book about child rearing, you think it'll sell?" I asked him.

"Point made!" laughed Mark.

"Not only that," I went on, "you and I have talked before about studies that back up the nagging feeling that music inside certain genres these days all sounds the same. It's become formulaic for obvious reasons, and this song is no different. This guy's 'instant hit' uses very familiar instrumentation, and a very familiar chord progression. I will, however, give him credit for at least putting the words *beer*, *girls*, *truck*, *boots*, *town*, and *road* in a slightly different order than usual."

"You're just jealous!" observed Mark.

"Probably," I admitted.

Just then, I heard a booming voice coming toward me, ringing out: "Docccc-torrr Derek!"

I looked up and there stood a mountain of a man, shod in cowboy boots, wearing a cowboy hat with a silver buckle on the front. "Romie, you old fart," I said, as I shook hands with his massive paw. "How the hell are ya?"

"Never better," he bellowed. "Good to see you again," he added. I introduced him to Mark, and asked him what he was drinking. "Chivas Regal," he announced, as our server arrived and took our order.

"You need to come up and do a song with us, Doc."

"You know, I might just do that," I replied as he walked away and I drifted off into thought. I had surprised myself a bit with the rapidity of my response, given that there was a time, not long ago, when I would have been less apt to make that statement so quickly. That was back when I had a primary care practice, and had more of a "public" presence.

Living in the same community where you practice medicine has some wonderful advantages, and also a few drawbacks. I had thoroughly enjoyed running into my patients at the grocery store, at ball games, on the street, and at church. Surprisingly—and delightfully—the great majority of them also respected my privacy when I wasn't at the office or on call, and instead contacted my partner on call with their urgent questions. This I considered a wonderful advantage, because a great part of being a primary care physician is being part of the community where your patients live.

The drawback part, admittedly a partial product of my own conception, related to patients' perception of what their doctor should be, how he should look, and how he should act. As it turned out, most of my patients who knew that I played in a rock band thought it was "cool" that their doctor actually had a life—while a couple who first encountered that fact when they saw me on a stage apparently mistook me for Mr. Hyde.

I've always been of the opinion that, in social situations, people should be able to behave like who they really are, no matter what they do for a living. Obviously there are limits to everything, as walking around your house with a pair of underwear on your head at night doesn't translate well to your job at the restaurant the next morning.

The rules of behavior for a doctor aren't quite so black and white. Obviously, if I want to smoke an occasional cigar with the boys, it would be best to do that at fishing camp and not out in public. If I am seen smoking that cigar even once in public, as a doctor, it is somehow seen as akin to endorsing that behavior regularly. I do understand that, and I try hard to refrain from the semblance, and the practice, of hypocrisy. Being human, I sometimes miss the mark, and when I, with a wink, tell patients "do as I say, not as I do," sometimes I am not lying. Fortunately, that is a relative rarity, though not so with everyone who practices medicine.

At least we have come a long way from the not-so-distant days when you could flip open the pages of *Life* magazine and see your doctor hawking a pack of Chesterfields. We all know a lot more now than we did then, though the Chesterfield image always makes me think of old Cal Bainor and chuckle.

Cal was an old time doc who worked in a small hospital in a neighboring community when I practiced primary care. Over time he managed to eat and drink himself into a behemoth of a man, which I suspect is how he managed to cope with the stress of what he did. I secretly admired the old fart, not for what he did to himself, but for the fact that the word *perception* was obviously not to be found in his dictionary. Anyone his size would stand out in a small hospital medical staff picture of twelve doctors, but the big smoking stogie clutched in his right hand really provided the finishing touch to—

"Dude! Hey dude!" Mark was practically yelling at me.

"Sorry man. I was drifted off in thought."

"No kidding," he said. "You were staring at the wall. I tried talking to you and got no response. Almost like you were having a petit mal seizure."

"I don't know," I said. "I've had a strange night, and there's something about this place that reminds me of something that I can't put my finger on right now . . ."

"You're not getting nauseated about going up on stage, are you?" Mark smirked.

We had both recently talked about a very famous rock 'n' roller who had admitted that he practically vomited every time he was about to go on stage.

"Hey, I realize that he needs to know the lyrics and guitar parts to several dozen rock songs—but so do us weekend warriors. He, however, plays ahead of tens of thousands of people. I, at most, have played ahead of a couple thousand people. But I still don't get it, and I realize for me it's probably a perspective thing."

"Meaning?" Mark asked.

"Meaning that I've considered that perspective against the perspective of what we do as physicians, because I've had experience with both sides. The best way I can compare the two in order to illustrate perspective is with a code blue situation. Showing up at a code blue cardiac arrest, to me, is kind of like walking on stage with your guitar just as the band starts your first song. You, however, have no idea what the song is, or what key they are doing it in. Nonetheless, you are expected to immediately discern that information and hit all the correct notes until, seconds later, the band makes an unannounced change into another unannounced song—and you do it all over again. Your punishment for not keeping up? Watching the bass player die. Moral of the story? From my perspective, the code is much more unnerving than the stage performance."

"True enough," Mark remarked.

"However," I finished, "my perspective is just that—mine. I have no idea how it must feel to get up in the morning and pin on a badge, or jump into your soldier suit, and in either case face the possibility of your *own* imminent death on a daily basis. *Those* are the guys—and gals—that really earn my respect."

The drinks had arrived, and Romie had walked back to our table. He was carrying a shot of whiskey in his hand. "This shot of Chivas is for you, Doc," he said.

"I don't drink that stuff," I countered, "unless it's mixed with something."

"Mix it with your beer then," he said, "and bottoms up on three. One, two, three," he boomed. For some reason I complied, and followed up the firewater with a swig of beer. "Now that wasn't bad at all, was it?" he laughed.

He slapped me on the back—hard. "Say, Doc, whatever happened to old Alex Gustavson? I know you've kept the Solid Gold Band going, but he started that thing up back in the Stone Age."

"Very sad to say," I replied, "he passed away a few years back."

"You couldn't keep him alive?" inquired Romie.

"There's only so much you can do with a guy who lathered butter on his steaks, crunched potato chips on his pizza, and drank Pepsi by the case, not to mention the two packs per day," I said.

"Didn't you two grow up in the same area?" Mark asked me.

"No—actually, Alex grew up in Duluth, moved here, and went to school at the University of Minnesota, though he stopped literally a couple of classes short of finishing his degree. I, on the other hand, *did* spend my childhood here, which is distinctly different from *growing up*—a process that I have continually tried to avoid."

Romie laughed. "Alex was really quite a character."

"Tell me about it," I said. "I really loved that guy, even with the difference in our ages. He gave me a shot playing with the band right out of high school, and I always appreciated that, even though we would at times fight like cats and dogs over the music that we chose to play."

Romie looked at me: "How's that?"

"Alex had a mind like a steel trap, except that musically and culturally it rusted shut in about 1968—and he was proud of it. You know how we all get to a point when we realize that past a certain earlier age in our lives, we can no longer identify songs on the radio or identify cars by their year and make as they drive by? Alex had taken that to a whole new level. He liked to brag that the last movie he ever saw was *Ben-Hur*, and he didn't take well to any 'new' music written after 1968. Despite that, he was a hell of a guy, and we had some really interesting times together. Hell, he even made it into the Rock and Roll Hall of Fame."

"What?" boomed Romie.

"No lie," I said. "When I visited the hall in Cleveland, I took one of our cards—with Alex's name on it—and stuck it in a crack in the wall on the second floor. He and the Solid Gold Band are both enshrined!"

Romie laughed again. "Being in the band business

long enough, we all get some really great stories to tell. What was the one again about Alex getting the radio stolen out of his truck?"

Just recalling the incident, I started laughing uncontrollably. I finally calmed down enough to blurt out, "I don't think you've ever heard this one, Mark, but you are going to love it."

I recalled to them being out at a gig at the Legion club in Faribault in the dead of winter several years previous. Alex had pulled the band trailer to the gig with his old Ford pickup. Being the old farm boy that he was, he never thought much about locking his doors, even though he had recently installed a fairly expensive new radio in the beast. At the end of the night, he came out to start the truck before we loaded up our equipment. He was extremely dismayed to find that someone had apparently calmly opened his unlocked door, and not so calmly ripped his new radio out of the dash.

Knowing that he had left his doors unlocked, and suspecting that insurance would more likely cover the cost of his radio if it were stolen during a break-in, he picked up a piece of pipe and smashed in his driver's door window. Why he did this at all, much less *before* he drove home that night, remains unknown. Suffice it to say, he froze his ass off on the trip back to Prior Lake that night. The next morning he got up and checked on his insurance coverage, and found out that he not only didn't have coverage for the radio, he also didn't have any glass coverage for the truck.

By the end of that story, Romie and Mark were both laughing so hard with me that I thought all three of us would fall out of our chairs. "The best thing about Alex was that he himself laughed his ass off in telling this story," I said. "If there is a heaven, the first thing I'm going to do if I get there is order up two steaks, a pound of butter, a bag of chips, a case of Pepsi, and find that old son of a bitch."

By then, the Legion was really starting to get packed with people.

"Looks like they like you guys around here, Romie," I observed.

"It's one of our favorite spots to play," he answered. "You know the drill, Doc. You find a spot you like, where the people like you, and you both keep coming back. No pretense here. It's a small place, but we do our thing and they have a good time. *Here*, it's about the music.

"We play bigger gigs from time to time," he continued, "but neither I nor any of my guys are willing to wear spandex or frizzy wigs or blow smoke up your ass doing some kind of schtick in order to stay on that circuit—or to put some scantily clad young lady out front to attract attention."

"I don't know," Mark winked, "*you* might attract quite a bit of attention if you came out to do the next set in a pair of fishnets."

"Christ, what is it with you doctors? You're not busy enough already that you need to set off a major epidemic of vomiting?"

The drummer was back on stage clicking his sticks,

Romie's cue to get back up on stage. "You comin' up, Doc?" he said.

"Why not?" I answered. By then I had finally calmed down somewhat from my strange experience in the ER—a testament to a little bit of time and a little bit of Chivas. "Do a couple of songs, Romie, and then I'll come up."

The band kicked off into a loud fast-tempo blues tune that the crowd clearly liked. Mark and I sat back in our chairs, sipped our beers, and enjoyed the show.

About two minutes into the song, I sensed movement on the chair that sat between Mark and me. I looked over, and it was obvious that some guy had decided that dancing on the floor wasn't enough fun for him, as he had chosen—beer in hand—to get up on top of our table and start dancing. I suspected that he had a couple of beers in him by that point.

I don't really mind someone having fun, but this obviously wasn't going to go well. Other people who have decided that the "party" is whatever and wherever and however they want it to be—ignoring everyone else—don't sit very well with me either. Nonetheless, I decided to give him a little bit of time to do his thing and then get back down. Right about then, he leaned down and said to me, "How ya doin' buddy?"

Not interested in appeasement at that point, I replied, "Get your ass off this table before you spill that beer on me and everyone else." I could hear him mumble something about "dancing on the table if he wanted to," and as I was about to stand up, he got down and went back toward the corner where his buddies were standing.

I am a doctor—which means that I often repair lacerations. I am also a man—which means that sometimes I want to cause them. By then, I was seething, tightening my fists, and getting angrier by the second. Accordingly, the inner voice in my cerebral cortex—the higher reasoning part of my brain that doesn't want to spend the rest of its life in prison after I punch a guy who then falls and hits his head and dies—kept telling me to calm down. My brain's limbic system, in its primitive way, had already wanted to have nothing to do with this kind of civility, and continued the fight against my cortex. I responded by looking over at Mark and saying: "Hey—I don't like having beer spilled on me."

Fred Astaire was over in the corner saving face with his buddies, mumbling something to the effect of: "He's not worth it."

I let him save face. I looked at Mark and added loudly, "Yeah, it's not worth it."

I stood up to stretch, but more so to let him know that I had about four inches and fifty pounds on him. I sat back down, we finished our beers, and they left. Practicing restraint ranks with one of the most difficult things men have to do. My cortex knows it was the right thing. My limbic system is still pissed off and refuses to let me off the hook.

After a couple of songs, Romie motioned me up to the stage. The lead guitarist had two nice axes on stands, a fine old Strat and a nice-looking Gibson SG copy. He handed me the Strat—nice guy. As I opened up my wallet, he asked me what I was looking for. "The thing all prepared guitarists carry around in their wallets," I answered.

"You mean a condom?" he said, chuckling, as I produced a lightweight Dunlop guitar pick.

I gave him the thumbs up after checking out the action on the Strat, which was tremendous. I was plugged into a Fender Blues Deluxe, with chorus, flange, and overdrive pedals at my feet. *Sweet*, I thought—*what a great setup*.

Romie ambled over and asked me what song I wanted to do. Having been in this position before as a stage guest of a band, as well as having myself invited musician guests to the stage, I was aware that we should stick with a good old standard—or at least a song with standard phrasing. As much as it was our goal to have fun with the upcoming song, our audience also deserved to hear a decent piece of music.

I gave him the name of a good old late eighties twelve-bar blues rock standard. He nodded his head: "We can kick some rock 'n' roll ass on that one."

What happened over the next four and a half minutes is still somewhat of a blur to me. I do clearly remember symbolically ripping page 973 out of Webster's Collegiate—the one with the definition of *perception* on it. Undoubtedly this drove me to repeatedly sing the line: "Don't hand me no lines, and go play with yourself."

What remains a blur is the guitar playing. At a basic level of explanation, most classic rock 'n' roll lead guitar solos are based on the pentatonic scale, with various additions or subtractions. Some refer to this as the blues scale. Listen to most anything by Chuck Berry and you will get the picture. The basic pentatonic scale is played over a four fret range on the guitar, but the neck of the guitar is long enough that the scale can be played in different forms in five different positions.

Accomplished guitarists have mastered playing the scale in multiple positions and can easily switch back and forth between these positions during a single solo. Besides mastering the scales, accomplished guitarists also use techniques like hammer-ons and pull-offs to play notes more rapidly than they could be played by striking a string with a guitar pick.

As a lead guitarist, I would personally refer to myself as adequate. In this case, I really am not doing that musician thing of not giving myself enough credit. I am adequate. With a bit of practice and the right song, I can rip off a decent lead guitar solo. Hell, I can even improvise a decent blues solo when called upon. Will I ever get any better? Like the golf thing, it may be a matter of how much time I have to invest, or maybe I'm confusing the guitar neck with a softball bat.

In any case, when it's my turn to lay down a solo, it usually revolves around the pentatonic scale in the basic position and sliding up twelve frets to the octave position—pretty standard stuff.

What happened during that four and a half minutes,

however, was anything but standard. Only later did I make the connection of similarity between what happened that day with my hands in the ER and what happened on the stage. During the two solos I played during that four and a half minutes, I watched in astonishment as my hands moved—and boy, did they move. I was doing scale positions that I wasn't sure existed. I was all over the place on the guitar neck, hitting runs of sixteenth notes interrupted only by an occasional screaming blues bend. By the end of the second solo, most of the crowd was standing, pounding their feet and clapping. I looked out at Mark, who was just sitting there with his jaw dropped open. He and I had played guitars enough together in the past for him to know that this was wildly atypical of me.

The song ended to a screaming round of applause, and I put the Strat down and walked back to the table and plopped into my chair. "What the hell was that?" Mark said incredulously.

"I have no freaking idea," I said. "I've been practicing a little more lately, but I have no freaking idea."

The band was on to their next song, and Romie gave me a big nod of approval as I walked past them and out to the deck behind the bar to get some air. I looked up into the starry sky and suddenly it came to me—what it was about this place that reminded me of something.

What I was reminded of was a striking similarity to another place a few miles down the road in the town of Shakopee that was no longer open. *The old Jug Lounge*, I thought.

This place smells just like it, and even looks a lot a lot like it.

The Jug Lounge, I thought—the location of my regret dream. It all flooded back to me.

Years previously, when I first started playing in the band with Alex, the Jug was one of our hotspots. I loved the place because it was laid back enough for us to do a steady stream of old classics, as well as some experimentation with other stuff that we wanted to try out. Even though Alex, as the bandleader, was pretty set in his ways regarding our regular song list, he was surprisingly open to trying out original music. Back then I was writing stuff in a number of different genres, apparently trying to find my muse. Turns out I had a decent talent for writing ballads—one, in particular, that figured heavily in my regret dream and in a copyright challenge that seemed to drag on forever.

I had written a whole album of original music with songs ranging from country, to rock 'n' roll, to ballads with a folk bent, and even a couple of original Christmas songs. Since the common thread among all of these tunes was life in the Midwest, I had decided that the theme of the album would be "flyover country." The standout ballad in the bunch was a song titled "Our Love Story (Is Ours Alone)."

I really loved the song and had used it as my example in the argument with my musical buddies over the long-standing question: What should be written first, lyrics or music? I favored to write lyrics first. These guys, still rockin' and rollin', had a wide range of opinions, and given their storied backgrounds, I respected them all.

When we eventually recorded the album, I picked their brains on the entire recording process. Charles Schoen (of the Del Counts), who had a big hit with "Come on Baby Let the Good Times Roll," had some great tips on the mixing process and the use of reverb, as did Pat (Teen King) Fitzgerald.

The Del Counts claim the distinction of being Minnesota's longest continually playing rock band, and, back in the day, Pat had the distinction of playing three different gigs in three different states within twenty-four hours. He opened for The Guess Who in two of them—during a period when he had done 479 gigs himself *in a calendar year.*

Since we were in Minnesota, no musical discussion could be considered complete without mentioning Prince, about whom we had heard some incredible stories from our band member Paul, who was out with him on his early tours. Including current band members Ron, Terry, and Bob, I felt fortunate just to get to hang around with so many talented guys. As fellow musician Jim Rieder accurately notes: "Surround yourself onstage with talent, and it'll make you look good."

Sitting in with other bands occasionally was also a treat, including Jim Donna's group, the Castaways. Their national hit, "Liar, Liar," had sent them on tour with the Beach Boys and was later featured in the movie *Good Morning, Vietnam.*

I was in the process of filling out the application for copyright for the album when we played the Jug Lounge on a cool night in November—the night before Thanksgiving, to be exact. We had messed around rehearsing the ballad during our regular band practice in Alex's heated garage the week before.

The night before Thanksgiving is always a huge bar night, as most people are off work the next day and ready to get in the holiday mood. That night was no exception.

We were having a great night playing our usual stuff, but as usual, our stuff did not contain much slow music, and for some reason, this crowd was in the mood. After we'd exhausted what we had, Alex whispered to me, "Why don't you play your ballad?"

I didn't jump at the idea because I wasn't sure that we, as a band, knew it well enough, and I knew in the back of my mind that the copyright had not been sent in yet. Alex pressed me again, and a little voice in the back of my brain, remarking on both of my reservations, squeaked, "You're at the Jug, dude. It's okay. Finish the set with the ballad."

So we did the song. I mentioned to the crowd that it was part of an album that I had written that the band was eventually going to record.

And thus began the events that gave rise to my dream . . . my recurrent dream . . . my dream of regret . . . my dream that would become more regular and more vivid as time went on.

Other than what ended up becoming a protracted copyright battle for the song, I certainly don't regret performing it. I don't even mind the recurrent dream, because I at least get to keep seeing her face. What I regret most deeply is my utterly stupid behavior that night.

Back then, I was at a point in my life where I had convinced myself that I was going to be different than all of those people in the small town where I grew up—different than those people who seemed to be sitting at the exact same barstool I saw them on when I had passed through town six months earlier. My answer to avoiding that fate was a two-pronged approach: education (finishing my residency), and the avoidance of any commitment that could interfere with it. I was perfectly happy composing love songs, but I was far from ready to live them out.

I started plucking out the guitar introduction to the song, and as I finished the eighth bar, I raised my face up to the microphone to sing. Standing barely fifteen feet away from me and staring directly into my eyes was the most incredible vision of beauty I had ever seen. Deep, beautiful brown eyes and gorgeous dark curly hair falling off of her shoulders. About five feet eight inches tall, with curves designed for a sports car—and staring directly into my eyes.

I froze—solid. I opened my mouth wide and all that came out was dead silence. After what seemed like an eternity, I felt a kick in the back of my pants. Instinctively, I began to play the guitar intro to the song again, and by the time I got to the end of the intro I was able to start singing, starting with the refrain, and the band followed. She was still looking into my eyes when Alex kicked up the stage lights, which illuminated the place and bounced back at me from the jewels on the cell phone case she was holding.

We have a story, a beautiful life song
Cause we've known the glory
Of a love that's oh so strong
It's ours together, though others have their own
Our love story
Is ours alone.

At the start, it took me by surprise
You knew it too, you could see it in my eyes
You know you're taken, when you can't eat or sleep
You know that you're in love so deep.

Growing together, when children came along
We knew forever, our love would stay this strong
We'd found the reason, what we were here to give
We'd found the place for love to live.

I repeated the refrain, did an instrumental, and followed with one more verse, followed by the refrain.

Throughout the years, our stories will be told
They'll warm our hearts, they'll warm our souls
They'll stay alive, not ever growing old
They'll touch us as they unfold.

We finished out the song with an eight-bar guitar instrumental. My voice never wavered—and I never took my eyes off of her. Other than breathing, she never moved a muscle. We were fifteen feet away from each other, but it felt to me like we were in the same body. That three minutes has played over in my dreams so many times, I could paint a perfect picture of it. The three minutes that followed are the part that haunts me.

We finished the song and she started walking toward me. I turned around to put my guitar back in its stand. I knew instinctively that she was standing at the edge of the stage, but I could not force myself to turn around and face her. I just stood there, in some weird sort of trance, facing the back of the stage. I really don't know how long I stood there, but I don't think it could've been more than a couple of minutes. When I finally turned around, she was gone.

I came to my senses and jumped off the stage and frantically began searching the place. I knew some of the regulars, so I described her and asked if anyone knew her or saw where she went. They had definitely seen her, but after the song was over, no one seemed to have any idea what had happened to her, and no one had recalled ever seeing her at the Jug before that night.

Three minutes, and all I'm left with is a mental recording that comes to me over and over in my dreams. As it turned out, on that night, someone else left the Jug—with an *actual* three-minute recording.

Chapter 8

It was too late to drive back up north that night, so I decided to go home and get an early start in the morning.

I turned the Blazer into my driveway, which was a 500-foot-long, winding asphalt path up to the house. I really didn't need to be renting a 6,000-square-foot house with a large storage barn, but I wasn't about to turn down the price tossed at me by Jack Graham. He and his wife and their two kids suddenly had to move out East when the network offered her an open slot in Boston. Jack pulled up roots for her career, and we were down another doc. Since we were operating on a rental basis, however, I wasn't convinced that the move was permanent. Jack was way too attached to this place.

I parked the Blazer, went in the side door, and trudged up the back staircase to the library over the garage. I flipped on the stereo and plopped down on the old leather couch. I loved the acoustics in this room, and therefore had taken the opportunity to set up the old quad stereo system that I had used in college. Steve always gave me a lot of good-natured crap for all of the "vintage" stuff I owned, from stereos to cars to my old speedboat and old snowmobiles.

There was a time—not all that long ago—when all I could afford was something "vintage," and I guess I had never really gotten over how cool owning stuff like that is. Growing up on the farm, I had also experienced first-hand what I consider to be true environmentalism—using something until its time had run its course, not discarding it merely because of the allure of purchasing something new. Of course, there was also the fact that we were "tight as bark to a tree" German farmers, but that doesn't sound anywhere near as romantic.

I figure that there has to be a point where you get happy with your toys, don't let them rule you, and just enjoy them—where you are okay being called an old fart if your idea of vintage doesn't add up to someone else's idea of cool. Where you realize that the best of something *ever* made may have already been made. Where reading and thinking and challenging yourself always trumps using your thumbs on a little box to shoot up humanity.

Everyone needs to find their own comfort point, but society's relentless advertising machine seems to keep driving us away from activities that require real thought. I'm not against advertising. I just wish people would be more discerning.

As to stereos, quad had been a passing fad in the 1970s and the precursor of surround sound systems, and it had always fascinated me. One of the reasons it had not caught on well was that most recorded music at the time was still on vinyl, and it was a real pain in the ass sometimes to get quad-recorded records to play the way they were supposed to. It was worth the effort, though, when you got Edgar Winter's *Frankenstein* literally rolling around the room through four strategically placed speakers.

The resurgence of vinyl now had many audiophiles looking back at old technologies. Kind of strange for me, a guy who often endeavored to stay a bit behind technology, now sitting at a sort of weird resurgent edge of it. I'll admit that my turntable is much less convenient than an iPod, but I'll challenge you on the sound quality any day.

Sansui had been the pioneer in the early development of quad systems and in early matrix quad technology. My college receiver was the very earliest of those—a basic sixty watt Sansui QR-500—and I still had it hooked to the same four bookshelf speakers I used in college.

It had been an extremely long day, and in less than five minutes I tipped over and was drifting off to sleep . . .

Call 239-6788, and order up a pizza that's really great!

Call 239-6788, and order up a pizza that's really great!

Call 239-6788, and order—

I sat up, still groggy, and tried to open my eyes. One more time I heard the words coming from the speakers:

Call 239-6788, and order up a pizza that's really great!

By then I got my eyes open and looked across to the bookshelf where the old Sansui was perched. I squinted to see the position of the analog dial marker. I hadn't looked closely when I had arrived home, but I thought that the receiver was tuned to 92.5—KQRS, the classic rock powerhouse of the Twin Cities. From where I sat, it now looked like the dial marker sat just below 101 on the dial. A fuzzy rendition of Edgar Winter's "Free Ride" was now coming through the speakers.

I got up, walked over to the receiver, and tried to adjust the dial to bring the channel in better. I gently turned the knob left and got nothing. I gently turned the knob right and got nothing. I gently turned the knob back and forth and got nothing. I turned the receiver off and went back to the couch.

"*Call 239-6788, and order up a pizza*"—*that's the old Pepper's Pizza commercial*, I thought. Even back in college we thought the jingle was stupid, and maybe it was, because the place closed—never to reopen—as I finished my junior year. KQZX 100.7, the college radio station on which they advertised, was shut down by the administration the next semester for DJ conduct "unbecoming of" the university.

I sat and tried to make some sense of what had just happened, but I was way too fried to think. Just another incident to add to the mix. *Nothing in this whole day made any sense*, I thought, as I tipped over on the couch and fell asleep. Deep sleep came quickly, accompanied by a disturbing dream . . .

Under a clear starlit sky in northern Minnesota, seven men were fast asleep in a bunkhouse. After the day's diet of beer and fried fish, the place was far from quiet, and hardly odor free. Another day on the lake had tired them out early, and they covered the fire and headed off to bed a couple hours before usual.

They were in the bunkhouse a good half an hour before

he showed up—sneaking up the edge of the driveway carrying two plastic five-gallon cans full of gas. He stepped off the driveway and put down the gas cans at the far edge of the deep ravine that separated the woods from the thousand feet of grassland that ran up to the bunkhouse. A small creek ran at the base of the ravine, which eventually trickled into the lake. There was enough moonlight for him to be able to see the cars that were parked near the bunkhouse. *Good*, he thought, as he spied the Mustang again—*he must be in that little building with the rest of them.* He had briefly seen the group of men earlier in the day, and hadn't been sure that he had seen the doctor. He had been told by Asmail, however, that the Mustang belonged to the doctor.

Soon it will be a tinderbox, he laughed to himself, and they will all burn. *Asmail will be extremely proud of me for this deed*, he thought, *as well as the previous deed of secretly mounting the tiny satellite digital video camera in the surface of the doctor's backpack.* He had snuck into the hospital with the help of a friend who had supplied him a housekeeping uniform and badge.

"Musha," Asmail had said, "the doctor must die. I would prefer that you could make it look like an accident, and this 'camp' he will be at would be the perfect place." Asmail had told him this two days earlier, when his surveillance had made him aware of where the doctor would be traveling.

If all had gone as planned, Musha would not have to be here putting plan B into place. *Why wait until the doctor ar-*

rives, Musha had thought, *when instead he could die en route?* Apparently, the tire slash just wasn't deep enough.

Musha turned off his small flashlight and pocketed it, letting his eyes totally adjust to the darkness, as he was too close to the bunkhouse to take the chance of the light being seen. He sat down on one of the plastic gas cans and went over his plan again in his head. He had been in the woods earlier in the day with a pair of Nikon Monarch high-powered binoculars before he had left, and he had seen the men sitting around the fire pit. A graduate student in communications at the state university was not supposed to know how to concoct a plan to carry out Asmail's wishes—and Musha didn't. He did, however, owe Asmail for his being in America, and therefore would do what he was asked to do, in the best way he was able to do it. He had gone back into Walker and gotten the supplies he needed.

Musha didn't know Asmail well, but it was obvious to him in their interactions that Asmail was deeply troubled, and perhaps on the edge of mental instability. He wasn't sure exactly what fueled Asmail's deep hatred for the doctor, but he knew it had something to do with an interaction they'd had years before that Asmail felt had destroyed his career aspirations. Musha wasn't about to press for more details. They had met in their native country before Musha's emigration to America, and since then they had communicated primarily by phone.

Musha was certain with the way the Americans were drinking that day that by now they would all be sound asleep and wouldn't be easily aroused. The lights were out in the bunkhouse and no one appeared to be moving. He would take the cans of gas and pour them around the foundation of the bunkhouse, saving enough to run a line of gas back to the fire pit. A drop of a lit match, and he would sprint back to his car, parked in a small field road at the edge of the woods.

He smiled at his ingenuity and stood up and removed the caps from the gas cans and stuck them in his pockets. He would carefully carry them that way to the bunkhouse so he could begin pouring gas around the foundation as soon as he got there.

Musha suddenly became aware of the pressure in his suprapubic area and realized that he hadn't urinated in several hours. He thought he had better relieve himself before the run that he would have to make back to his car. He didn't want to turn his flashlight back on, so he turned around, took a couple of steps, and let fly. He turned back around and took a couple of steps as he yanked upward on his stuck zipper. It didn't budge as he took one more step and walked right into the plastic gas can on the right. He could hear it fall and start to slide, and while simultaneously hissing "Damn," he grabbed for the can on the left, only succeeding in knocking it over as well.

He fumbled in his pocket for the small flashlight and snapped it on. Both gas cans were sliding toward the bottom of the deep ravine, spilling gas in their wake.

"*Kesafat*," he hissed at himself, "you idiot!" He quickly

thought about trying to climb down the ravine and retrieve the cans, but it was just too steep. He could walk through the woods to a less-steep part of the ravine, but by the time he got there and walked back, the gas cans would probably be almost empty anyway.

"*Kesafat*," he hissed again, as he used his flashlight and found a rock to sit on. He turned off the light, put his head in his hands, and tried to decide what to do next. Unzipping a small pocket on the left arm of his jacket, he pulled out a pack of Bahmans and lit one up. He took several deep drags off of the cigarette and realized—disgustingly—that he would have to drive back into Walker to get more supplies and start over.

He took one last drag and flicked the cigarette out of his fingers. In that very instant he realized what he had just done. He had no idea where the cigarette had gone, but *What were the chances?* he thought.

Musha flipped the flashlight back on and walked to the edge of the ravine.

Flames were already making their way up the side as he turned and ran toward his car, suspecting that his days as an assassin were over . . .

I rolled over on the couch to a more comfortable position and rapidly fell back into deep sleep, and into another disturbing dream . . .

A single camouflaged figure positioned himself and

his Bushmaster AR-15 assault rifle in the direction of an oncoming vehicle. It had begun to drizzle, and he was wet and cold, and, above all, disgusted. However, his spirits were quickly brightened as the fog momentarily cleared, and he realized—through the lens of his high-powered binoculars—that his target was actually *coming to him*! It couldn't get any better than this!

I should've known better than to entrust this job to Musha, thought Asmail. *The stupid fool screws it up, and then goes into hiding*. The thought of his rapid-fire ordeal of Kish Air to Paris, Air France to New York, Delta to Minneapolis, and a bumpy ride up to this hellhole made Asmail nauseated. He had been on his way here anyway—but to celebrate, not to do the job himself. Musha's frantic call as he landed in New York had quickly changed that—but at least Musha had put him in contact with an associate who supplied the rifle.

Now, the job needed to be done before anyone got suspicious—it really didn't matter anymore whether it looked like an accident. The only thing that quelled his nausea was the knowledge that in a matter of minutes, the bastard would be dead, and his big friend could burn in hell right along with him.

The fog had settled back in and given him excellent cover, even more than the small patch of trees that Musha hadn't managed to burn down. It would make his targets harder to see, but if he needed to walk right up to them and put the barrel right between their eyes before he fired, it would not bother him in the least. *I may do that anyway*, he thought, *just to see the fear in their eyes before I pull the trigger—just compensation for what that son of a bitch did to me.*

Asmail now could clearly overhear the loud conversation of the men as they shut down their vehicle. *Stupid American men,* he thought—*pining over a woman!* He could take as many women as he wanted—whenever he wanted. *With the first clearing of the fog again, I will put both of these two out of their misery . . .*

I rolled over on the couch once more, didn't dream again for the rest of the night, and unfortunately didn't recall the details of either dream the next morning.

Chapter 9

Sunlight streaming through the east window eventually gained enough energy to wake me up. My first sensation was that of my mouth, informing me of its apparent two-week stay in the Gobi desert. Immediately following was my bladder attempting to kick its way out of my abdomen. I complied with its call and made my way back to the library. Having no idea what time it was, I unzipped my coat pocket and pulled out my phone.

Staring me in the face was the announcement of six missed phone calls—all from Schmitty. *What the hell*, I thought, until I realized that the phone was on mute. "Damn it," I muttered out loud, when I remembered that I had switched off the phone when the Bird Dogs band had started their first set.

I immediately rang up Schmitty, who sounded understandably perturbed. "Sorry man," I said, "my phone was on mute so I didn't hear it ringing."

"No shit," he said. "Well, you're not going to believe what happened up here."

"What's that?" I asked.

"Almost the entire woods, and I mean the entire effing woods, completely burned down last night."

"What?" I said. "What?" I repeated loudly.

"You heard me, man," he said. "Fortunately, everyone

and everything here in camp is okay, buildings, cars and all."

"What the hell happened?"

"We have no idea," he said. "We're absolutely sure that the campfire was out before we went to bed last night, and as usual we covered the fire ring with the heavy metal plate that we always use. Besides, there are absolutely no burn marks anywhere near the campfire site."

"God, that's crazy," I said. "I'm just glad that everyone is okay. I'm about to jump in the Blazer and head back up. Is there anything you need me to bring?"

"Naw, you know the drill. We have about four weeks' worth of food sitting here, and enough beer to drown Paul Bunyan, so I think we're good."

I took a quick shower, jumped back in the Blazer, and headed down the driveway to go back north. I had been operating like I was on autopilot since getting the call from Schmitty. Halfway down the driveway I hit the brakes and put the truck in park.

Stop for a minute, I told myself. *Think—think! Think about what happened yesterday, and what happened the day before that. You haven't even taken a minute to try to process any of this.*

I turned the engine off, got out of the Blazer, and sat down on the edge of the driveway. It was an absolutely beautiful spring day. *All right*, I told myself, *let's try to put this in perspective. Two days ago, you were sitting in a tree stand and tipped your head back and felt like you were in some strange sort of vortex. Yesterday you did a shift in the ER and were some strange sort of diagnostic superstar, and then, there was that guitar-playing bonanza last night. What the hell is going on?* I let my mind wander and let the cool breeze blow across my face until the obvious connection struck me.

When I tipped my head back in that tree stand, what was I thinking about? I was thinking about musicians and how they downplay their talents, and I was thinking about my diagnostic skills as a physician. "Holy shit!" I said out loud.

I ran back to the truck, grabbed my phone, and dialed up Schmitty. "Listen man, I need to ask you something. You remember me talking to you about being in the tree stand, right?"

"I do," he said.

"Is that tree still with us, or did it go down in the fire?"

"That whole section of the woods is one big pile of ash and a few stumps," he said.

"Dammit," I said.

"What's the problem?" Schmitty asked, and then quickly added, "Ooh, I see the problem. You want to get back up in that tree stand, but now you have no tree and no stand."

"Could you get me close to where that tree stood?"

"Close maybe, but no guarantees."

I pulled the phone away from my ear, turned and looked at it, and put it back up to my ear. "We need a cherry picker," I yelled into the iPhone.

"Geez man, don't break my eardrum," came the reply.

"Sorry, Schmitty—got a bit excited."

"Did you say you needed a cherry picker? What the hell are you going to do, harvest apples?"

"It's not what I am going to do, it's what *we* are going to do."

"Should I be excited by this idea, or should I start writing my will?" he said.

"Both," I replied, attempting humor, but not realizing at the time how close to the truth I was.

As I drove out the driveway and headed back toward camp, I told him about my experiences of the day before, and then filled him in on my plan. Despite consciously staying a step or two behind some technologies (to avoid becoming a slave to them), I did have an up-to-date phone. These days, who can't? I hate planned obsolescence, but at least it keeps me up to date in a couple of areas, like laptops and cell phones.

I told Schmitty it had struck me that while sitting in the vortex tree two days earlier, I had been messing around with my phone and had used Google Maps to pin the spot. I could get us back to the exact spot where the tree stood, but I needed a way to get us twenty feet up in the air—hence, the cherry picker.

"I know this guy," Schmitty said.

"Now there's a surprise," I muttered.

"Doc, do something really difficult for you, and just shut up a minute and listen to me," he said. I complied—briefly.

"There is a guy about five miles from here named Diggie—"

I couldn't help myself as I interrupted him again: "Really—Diggie?"

"Yeah, Diggie," he said. "Got the nickname from the fact that he used to own an excavating business before he bought a bar up here, just down the road from us."

"Original," I laughed.

"He kept a couple of pieces of equipment from the old business, and for some reason, one of them was a cherry picker. I have no idea what he used that old thing for anyway, but it is still sitting in the weeds back behind the bar. I was over there not that long ago, and he told me that he had just fired the thing up, so obviously it still runs."

"I would be ever so indebted if we could figure out a way to be able to use the thing. How about free prostate exams for everyone?"

"Given some of our previous experiences, Doc," he said, "and knowing how some of your adventures end up turning out, I can feel that finger already."

"*My* adventures?" I inquired.

"Yes, *your* adventures," he said. "For example, need I remind you that your last adventure ruined the sport of snowmobiling forever for Steve?"

"That was a total accident," I said. "If he can't handle submerging two snowmobiles so deeply in a creek that they needed to be pulled out with a wrecker, that's his problem," I laughed, and hung up the phone. I realized then that we hadn't talked about why it was so important for me to get back up into the vortex so quickly, but we had talked about my regret dream before, and it wouldn't take him long to put two and two together.

On the trip back up, I tried desperately to keep my mind off of what had happened at camp, and what I was going to do when I got there. I decided to take a slightly different route to help distract me.

The first part of the trip didn't take me back to the old hometown, but my mind did. This time, it wandered back to the halls of the old high school. It didn't take me long after graduating from there—actually, right after I started college—to realize what a valuable education that small school had given me.

I had originally decided to be a college music major and was all set to go to a small school in South Dakota with a great music program. My parents had decided that that particular school's religious affiliation was not in line with that of our family, and literally at the last minute pushed me toward a Catholic university. I rebelled and took the first semester off, losing my scholarship in the process. I ended up enrolling at the Catholic university midyear, for which I ended up paying full boat, because entrance scholarships had already been paid out. In the end, however, it turned out to be an excellent choice. It was there that I quickly realized how incredible my small high school and many of its teachers actually were, starting with my beloved science teacher, Mr. Reitman.

The man was incredibly intelligent, and it was obvious during every minute that you spent in one of his classes that he absolutely loved what he was doing. He made science so much fun that you couldn't help wanting to soak up every bit of information that he passed on. He would get that little-kid smile on his face whenever he would do an experiment that went right, and most of them did, with only an occasional semblance of the Tacoma Narrows Bridge collapse.

Of course, the ones that didn't go right ended up in the annals of local folklore. Back in the day, in this small school, he and most of my other teachers basically did what they wanted, and I and the rest of my fellow students ended up richer for it—and with some great stories to tell.

The man had a penchant for cooking up contact explosives, and every one of his chemistry classes got treated to a yearly batch that he made and subsequently exploded in the hallway outside of his classroom. A feather on the end of a ten-foot metal pole served as the contact point. The ritual went on without fail for a number of years, until one fateful spring when the batch simply refused to explode. Reitman was crestfallen. He scooped up the batch, opened the back door leading into the school, and dumped it out over one of those rubber honeycomb mats used ahead of entry doors. Apparently the batch just needed a little more time to mature, because the next day a group of visiting "dignitaries" from somewhere else in the district came to visit, and, of course, entered the school through that same door. You can imagine the rest.

I barely went a day in any of my college chemistry classes without thinking of his application of humor to the process of science in its attempt to explain the universe. After I was dubbed "The Table Chemist" in my college intro course—knocking over my own vial of substrate and scooping it, and whatever else was on the table, into another vial to run the experiment—I recalled his evocation of "the law of the variable constant and the constant variable." "Finagle's Law"—the act of changing the universe to fit the equation—aptly applied as well.

In our small school, the science teacher taught chemistry, physics, and biology. I took the first two, and was allowed to audit biology as a senior by just sitting in and absorbing the class, made up of sophomores. This went well until one day when Mr. Reitman asked class members to read sections out of the biology text. The poor girl reading that day was completely unaware of her pronunciation error, and of me sitting directly behind her, pinching myself 'til I damn near bled in order to keep from exploding with laughter. Problem was, the phrase in the section she read was being repeated over and over, and I eventually excused myself to go to the bathroom, never to return to the class. Since that day—the day of "the one-celled orgasm"—I've never been able to think of an amoeba and keep a straight face.

Down the hall was the English classroom, the home of Mr. Bogevan. He was also my high school speech coach, so he knew what I was capable of concocting. I distinctly remember the day I got one of my English papers back from him, presented to me flipped over on my desk. I turned it back over, and staring at me—in bold red ink—were the words *Bullshit! Bullshit! Bullshit!* written all across the front page.

Now I could have been "offended," or complained that my "self-esteem" had been viciously attacked—or I could have done what I did, which was to sit there and laugh out loud because the man was spot on in his criticism. Neither Bogevan, nor anyone else since, has been able to completely cure my verbosity, but his critique that day at least inspired me to move in the right direction.

At the very end of the hall was the combined band and choir room. This was the blessed retreat where most of my friends and I hung out, and, without a doubt, what we did there saved many of us. Recounting the things we did as high school music students in that school still amazes me.

We had arrived as sophomores to face Bindven and Breen, the new instrumental and choral music teachers—both of whom appeared to be tough taskmasters, especially the instrumental guy. The choir teacher was a doll, but it was obvious that we weren't going to push her around either. Bindven figured that out pretty quickly as well—the doll part—and, suffice it to say, they eventually got married.

When it came to letting us off the hook, these two had apparently been hired to take no prisoners, and they succeeded in drawing out every bit of the talent deeply buried in our small-town bodies. In no time, we had a music theory class where we created our own original compositions to perform, and where we also did our own arrangements of the music that we performed at our concerts. Not satisfied with that, or the lavish musicals we produced, Bindven decided that we were going to write, produce, and perform our own original musical—which we did, and quite successfully.

By the time we graduated there was one more challenge before the two left town, and a la the old movie *Summer Stock*, a handful of us transformed an old building in town into a dinner theatre, with Bindven in the lead role in the production. We, of course, had as much fun messing around after rehearsals as we did during them. Most of us were now high school graduates—almost adults. Perhaps that is the reason why I really didn't get embarrassed when someone saw my ass during a costume change backstage—but it was more likely because they had already seen it so many times during our "mooning" cruises after rehearsals.

Cruising was the mainstay of entertainment for the youth of the town—before, after, and sometimes during partying. Old George Setzer, the town cop, eventually threw up his hands and went all Stockholm Syndrome. To keep appearances, though, he would pull over the occasional car, stuffed with eight teenagers.

The exchange would go something like this: "Where are you partying tonight?"

"We're not."

"Well, don't party in town tonight, 'cause the county squad is coming through town."

The next week the exchange would go something like this: "Where are you partying tonight?"

"We're not."

"Well, don't party out in the country tonight, 'cause the county squad is coming through there."

As the story goes, old George eventually succumbed to his own demons and disappeared, to be discovered a few days later sitting in his squad in the middle of a Nebraska field drinking a beer, sirens on and red lights flashing.

We never had to worry about the county squad finding us out on Molly's Hill, because it was so well hidden. About a mile from Saint James Church was a tiny winding field road that went up around a rim of trees and deposited us on a flat spot where cars could be parked, a few beers could be popped, and the conversation could begin.

As conversations went, we had some doozies. They later remained so indelibly burned in my mind that "The Molly's Hill Boys" became the opening song on our "flyover country" album. It was the only song we recorded digitally on an album that had otherwise been done completely in old-school analog.

The Molly's Hill crew was primarily made up of my fellow farm boy friends, and, of course, we talked about girls and school, and bragged about our cars. It got really interesting when subjects were ventured into that were much deeper than farm boys sitting on the hoods of their cars in the middle of a field would be expected to go.

We debated the state of the world, and the meaning of

life, and the most interesting and potentially divisive subject of all—religion. We came from surprisingly diverse religious backgrounds, which led to some interesting arguments. As I remember, the most explosive of these centered around the age of the earth—the "scientific" camp versus the "strict interpretation of the Bible" camp. I simply could not be convinced that the earth is less than six thousand years old, and if old nuns drank beer, I could have eventually lured the perfect debating partner up to Molly's Hill to settle the issue once and for all.

Sister Carrie Green taught a number of advanced biology classes at Saint John's, but "Ma" Green's love of teaching kept her in the general biology classroom as well. I checked into her class midyear, which was a bit awkward, but at least they had already covered the amoeba.

As with her class, I also jumped midyear into calculus, which was when I discovered how well my small high school had prepared me. Getting an A earned me credit for the first half of the year that I had missed. Testing out of a number of other subjects, taking classes through independent study, and taking a couple summer school classes the first two years—as well as some creative manipulation of degree requirements—earned me a bachelor's degree in natural science, one in social science, and a minor in economics in the space of five semesters. Throw in concert band, jazz band, concert choir, Axel T's men's choir (from which singing sensation Tonic Sol-Fa was spawned), and intramural sports, and I didn't sleep much—but it was a blast!

Sister Green carried an incredible resume: Fulbright

Scholar, researcher at the Max Planck Institute in Germany, student at Woods Hole Marine Biological Laboratory—the lady had cred. She also had guts.

Within the first week, the subject of creationism vis-à-vis evolution came up. *An interesting juxtaposition for a nun-scientist*, I thought. Her take on the subject made me realize instantly that at Saint John's, I was in exactly the right place.

She made no effort to justify the tenets of either position, but instead examined both completely, and concluded that they were not mutually exclusive. Who is to say that a biblical "day" is twenty-four hours, she asked, instead of eons? Who is to say that creation was not allowed to happen by evolution, she wondered, instead of instantaneously?

Why, oh, why didn't she drink beer?

I looked at my watch, surprised that it was already 11:30 a.m., and upset that I had slept in so late. Since there was still a three-and-a-half-hour trip ahead of me, I decided that I'd better grab some lunch. I really wasn't in the mood to eat in the car, and despite being on vacation, I was making a concerted effort to avoid fast food.

I pulled into Shakopee and headed toward Dangerfield's Restaurant. I passed the old Jug Lounge on my left, sadly now closed down. Two blocks later, a left turn brought me to my destination.

Dangerfield's was a culinary institution, nestled up against the backwaters of the Minnesota River, and I was a regular. I stepped in the front door and was greeted with a loud "Hello, Doctor," from Gus, the owner. He led me back to a table in the raised seating area overlooking the "Millpond" and its collection of winged wildlife.

It appeared that outside seating on the patio was closed that day, and when I asked why, Gus told me that they were in the process of replacing "the state bird barrier." Peering around the corner, I noticed three workmen on scaffolding busily installing new mosquito netting.

I have eaten at a lot of fine restaurants over the years, but this place always draws me back. I ordered up the London broil flank steak, a salad, and the incredible popover that came with it. The only thing better—had I not been driving—would have been the addition of a glass of Merlot.

Soon I was on the road again, headed toward the Twin Cities. I rolled into Savage, home of Dan Patch—world's fastest pacing horse at the turn of the century. Family lore had it that my grandfather had owned a relative of Dan Patch that was fast enough to race the trains of the time.

Since I knew I'd be passing through, I had brought my 1960 Fender Stratocaster with to drop it off for a tune-up by the only guy that I trusted to work on such a relic—a guy who bought and sold classic guitars across the country.

I pulled into Valley Music, walked in, and was greeted by Gene.

"How's it going, Doc?" he said.

"Not bad," I answered. "Dropping off the old Strat for a tune-up, and then I'm headed out of town."

He asked where I was headed, and being a fisherman

himself, we talked a bit about the sport and eventually got around to why I was taking time off in the first place.

Gene was a guy who knew a tremendous amount about guitars, and more about people. "I'll tell you why we are so polarized," he said. "I'm not here to take shots at people, but politicians are the ones who keep fanning the flames. I was out to dinner with a friend of mine recently whose political persuasion is definitely 180 degrees away from mine. During conversation he started touting the usual party narrative, and then proceeded to tell me how far apart he *knew* the two of us would be on the issues."

"What happened?" I asked.

"I told him to grab a napkin and start writing down his positions, and I would do the same. He took my bet that I believed our ideas would be a lot closer than he thought."

"And?" I said.

"And—he paid for dinner."

Back on the road, I passed Savage Sound, owned by a guy who had played drums with us for a while and who also created custom amplifiers that he sold to some of the best musicians in the business.

Feeling guilty, I called Schmitty: "Sorry, man," I said. "I had to stop for lunch, so I'll be a little bit late."

"And that should shock me?" he laughed. He said that it was beginning to cloud up, and that rain was expected. I chastised myself again for getting a late start and hoped that the weather wouldn't interfere with my plans. In this state, the weather allows no one to become complacent.

Unpredictable weather does interfere with a lot of plans here in Minnesota, and predictable weather is also responsible for a lot of plans—often to get out of state for a bit by the end of winter. Winter in Minnesota is beautiful—if you grew up in Minnesota. Skiing and ice fishing and sledding and snowmobiling and skating are wonderful outdoor activities, but even the greatest diehard natives among us are ready for a break by the time March rolls in. Around then, about half the state moves to Fort Myers Beach for a week. We trade snow for a car trip down Estero Boulevard that lasts long enough to write half the great American novel.

Spring in Minnesota is a short snowmelt followed by the reawakening of foliage, and the half of the state that didn't escape winter by heading to Florida is ready for it to be over by then. Hot summer and warm fall here are fantastic, especially the fall color show put on by our myriad deciduous trees. Winter rolls around again, and the national media rolls out a few shots of a blizzard hitting the state that further solidify the notion to many in the South that the footage they are seeing must've been shot here in August.

It was still sunny here in the southern part of the state, which was not a surprise. Minnesota runs 407 miles from southern border to northern border, so the differences in its weather forecast often resemble that of two different northern European countries, especially in the springtime—and the rapid weather changes here are often inextricably tied to the medical emergencies we face.

I thought of this as I crossed into Saint Paul and rolled past my old residency hospital—also a place of fond remembrance when it came to interesting teachers and interesting experiences. We all learned a helluva lot in that old edifice. Some of us learned a helluva lot more when we hiked up our moonlighting shorts and headed to outstate ERs, where we got spanked by just about any kind of weather—and medical emergency—you could imagine. Too bad I didn't have a vortex back then . . .

Old man winter provided the backdrop early on in my training, about five months into my internship year, when on the night before Thanksgiving, all of Saint Paul was shut down in a massive snowstorm. This was before hospitalists stayed overnight in hospitals, and before obstetricians kept someone stationed in the hospital at all times.

The place was being run by me—the intern on call covering obstetrics; the resident—tied up with an emergency in the house; and another intern—tied up with the ER doc. No one else could even make it into the hospital, except a woman who lived very near the hospital, probably driven into labor by the storm itself.

She and her husband arrived, and it was obvious that she was in full-blown labor. Problem was, she was only twenty-eight weeks along and the baby was double footling breech—both feet first. A baby presenting this way at twenty-eight weeks could be enough to make even a seasoned obstetrician shit his pants. Fortunately for me, I was still green enough to not have developed the full defecation response, and I got the baby delivered and stabilized by the time an ambulance was able to plow through the drifts to pick up and deliver the child to the children's hospital.

As I thought about my teachers here, I realized how much times had changed in the relatively short span since I had completed my residency. Without a doubt, these days someone would work themselves into a lather to find some sort of offense in the ever-so-descriptive, yet ever-so-funny, patient chart comments left by my internal medicine mentor, Dr. Dell Vogler.

I recalled being on patient rounds one day early in my internship year. Vogler was leading the charge and exhibiting a sense of humor described by his colleagues as "drier than a popcorn fart." He was brilliant and he was kind, but not so kind as to let you slip by unscathed if you weren't completely aware of what was going on with your patients or the various nuances of their medical conditions. We thus hung on his every word and deed, and each and every one of his teaching pearls.

We had just finished seeing an elderly gentleman, sound asleep, who had a small white pill stuck to his face just below his lower lip. He slept right through our exam of his heart and lungs, and after discussing his case, we went back to the nurse's station. Vogler left a written chart note, and we stared over his shoulder at the proclamation: "Patient exhibits classic I.T.O.C. sign." He signed his note and we walked away, none of us knowing what a classic I.T.O.C. sign was, and none of us willing to ask. Curiosity eventually bested our fear of appearing ignorant, so we inquired. "Inderal tablet on chin," came the response.

On a different point in the spectrum, there was Billy Minola, an old-time family doc who was fiercely loyal to his patients, and fiercely stuck in his ways. He had practiced medicine for a *long* time and had remained just as sharp as he was sarcastic. We never quite figured out if he hated technology, didn't understand it, or didn't think he needed it. Often, when we ordered a test on one of his patients, he would pummel us with: "CAT scan, bat scan, rat scan, mouse scan."

One day I got called in for a sit-down in the residency director's office, after I made the mistake of keeping one of Billy's patients alive. I was an intern working in the ER, and, as was the custom back then, trying to run the place by myself without bothering the resident in the house, who could have given me the lowdown on Billy. I hadn't met Billy yet, but I was about to.

One of his patients came in in full cardiac arrest, without a resuscitation status on the chart. I therefore pulled out all the stops, which included pulling out a long intracardiac needle, which I used successfully to get the patient's heart restarted. The patient made it up to the ICU, where he existed vegetatively for another week before succumbing. Billy was livid, and I was pissed for being called on the carpet.

Since that day, I've had plenty of my own experiences, on both ends of the spectrum. I have been involved in new born resuscitation where the week that the parents got with their child before choosing to pull the plug was truly a divine gift. I've also done resuscitations on the other end of the spectrum at the family's request, where they later were sometimes thankful, and sometimes regretful.

Thinking back on my residency experience, and my experiences since, I have come to a few conclusions. First: Billy was a stubborn old curmudgeon—but that in no way made him a bad doctor. In fact, his fierce loyalty to his patients made him a *better* doctor than many I've run across since. Second: Billy notwithstanding, doctors in general rely too much on technology. Third: Billy's patient should have had a resuscitation status on his chart, as we later learned from his family that the patient would have favored that we not pull out all the stops. Billy was right that it was a shame this patient's family had to endure the week they did—but it could have been avoided.

As a doctor, it is impossible to be present at all times to represent your patient's wishes if they have not represented, or cannot represent, their own. Accordingly, the fact that we spend the great majority of all Medicare dollars in the last three months of patients' lives is an issue we need to stop avoiding in our national debate. We, however, cannot seem to bring ourselves to truly debate *any* of the tough questions—and why should we, Dick Johnson would say, when we can just keep borrowing our way into oblivion and spending our problems away? Another good case for term limits.

The familiar ring of my cell phone pulled me out of my set of deep thoughts about medicine and potentially into another: the ER was calling.

Chapter 10

"I'm on the way back up north, Kath," I answered. "What's happening?"

"That's exactly what I was planning to ask you—about you—again. You still haven't told me what in hell is going on with you, Mann, and you know me. I'm going to hound your ass until you tell me. But that's not why I called. I wanted to let you know that Maude is doing great. She had diffuse four-vessel coronary disease that couldn't be stented, so they bypassed her. And about that, how the hell did you know to call a code sixty-eight before you even saw her EKG? There's something strange . . ."

I made a few static-like sounds near the phone and then answered: "You're breaking up, Kath. I must be losing reception."

"Losing reception, my ass," I heard her yell as I shut off my phone. Keeping her in the dark wasn't my intention, but I didn't really know what to tell her—yet.

Zipping past the northern suburbs toward beautiful northern Minnesota, I again began to wonder what I would face if I was able to get back into the vortex. I was simultaneously excited and anxious about the prospect, and more than a little concerned about the effects that it might have on me—but not so much that I wasn't going back in. I again tried to move my mind on to something else.

The highway sign I was coming up on told me to keep right if I was headed to Duluth, so I stayed left. I had made the trip to Duluth so many times when I was in med school that I'm surprised I didn't just steer the car that way automatically.

I had spent the first two years of medical school at UMD in Duluth, before transferring—as was the rule—to the University of Minnesota in Minneapolis for years three and four. UMD had a fantastic reputation for attracting students that were interested in primary care. They also had an incredibly personable dean, Tim Loeffler, who made it clear from day one that we were all "family" now, and that we would all get through this together. We didn't realize until later that that included his accompanying us down to a local watering hole called The Reef after particularly grueling days as first-year students dissecting cadavers. We got along great together, even after the "toga incident."

Medical students take a board exam to test the basic science knowledge taught to them during their first two years. There is generally a lot of study prep for the exam, though in Duluth our scores generally beat the pants off of the other two medical schools in the state, so we knew that we had been learning the right stuff all along. Nonetheless, it was a big test, and everyone got worked up for it, and everyone was ready to let off steam when it was over.

It was tradition that the dean held a reception for faculty and students in his backyard after the test. Just to be clear, the invitation to this event was not the only invitation

I have ever misread. I apparently had misread invitations before this event, and I certainly have misread invitations after this event—being convinced that many of them were indeed invitations to toga parties.

Somehow, the fact that I have shown up at multiple parties being the only guest with a white sheet wrapped around me and a plastic laurel on my head has never convinced me to stop doing it, and this day was no exception. "When in Rome" certainly must apply when you're dressed like a Roman, and on this particular day I acted the part.

Unfortunately, after the appropriate amount of debauchery, I didn't just leave and stumble past the Colosseum on my way home. Something in my head convinced me that the garden hose wrapped up next to the house needed to be put to use. Perhaps I was convinced that all of the guests in attendance were actually plants, because I proceeded to water each and every one of them.

As my date stalked away, remorse apparently set in, and I tried in vain to catch up to her. She gained repudiation by looking at me and saying, "Keep walking until you get at least half a block ahead of me." I haven't been able to get any closer to her since.

I was now driving through a beautiful rolling area, a bit of a break in the pine trees. Off to my left was a small lake, its surface as bright and still as a mirror. I could see in the distance a huge stand of pines rimming the back side of the shoreline, but the entire near side of the lake was devoid of vegetation. There were but two houses on a five-hundred-foot or so stretch of shoreline. The second house had a very weathered-looking, narrow wooden dock that ran about thirty feet out into the water, and as I passed, a young boy ran full speed down the dock and jumped off the end, creating a large cannonball splash in the water. Ripples from the splash rapidly reverberated outward across the mirror-like surface.

Something about the scene looked familiar. It took me a minute to realize that this small lake looked a lot like a bay back on much larger Prior Lake, where that same type of cannonball splash was done a few months earlier, but into water barely above freezing.

The Polar Plunge is a fund-raising creation of Special Olympics of Minnesota in which crazed, cabin-fever-afflicted Northerners secure monetary pledges for the cause, dress up in whatever wild costume their spouse will allow them to leave the house in, and jump into water that is less than half a degree from being an ice cube. Prior to this, huge blocks of ice have to be cut and removed from the lake to create a hole large enough for those not faint of heart to leap into.

Teams, of course, end up being created for such an event. Those teams, of course, end up meeting somewhere—before the event, to garner courage—and after the event, to brag about what a "piece of cake it was" and to consume even more liquid courage. In my case, we started out at T. J. Hooligans in Prior Lake, a bar and restaurant that most certainly is the local equivalent of Cheers. The atmosphere was interesting and relaxed, with everything from an antique Whizzer motorbike to a guitar signed by the Solid Gold Band hanging from the ceiling. John and Dave run the place and will whip you up a Mexican meal that you will never forget.

After a couple of necessary trips to the urinal, everyone boarded the bus for the trip to the lake, and the jumping began. Costumes really were optional, but seemed to be highly encouraged. Ever vigilantly the iconoclast physician, mine included a pair of jumper cables draped over my neck, hooked to a single D-cell flashlight battery with a sign that read: "HMO Defibrillator."

After the jump, the outside run back into the warming tent, and the sticky redressing procedure, we reboarded a bus and headed back into town. We drove past Edelweiss Bakery, a delightful European style boulangerie, and ended up at the local VFW. The VFW was a sponsor of the plunge and many other civic activities, and a damn good place to have a steak and hear some great music.

Across the street sat the Extra Innings Saloon, sponsor of my former league softball team. I had played for them before med school and on into residency. I still occasionally get reminded by ex-teammates of a postgame night there that I barely recall—something about drinking champagne out of a woman's high-heeled shoe the day I got my med school acceptance letter.

By the time we hit the VFW I had warmed up again, which was a surprise, because jumping into that water was more of a shock than I was expecting. This was mainly because I had endured what I thought was a much more trying cold water experience when I was in med school, which was of course a few years previous.

We had a physiology professor who for some reason—sadism or otherwise—had decided to replicate old war experiments that dealt with the body's ability to withstand exposure to the cold. Some of these actually had commercial relevance, like the one I was involved with, which tested clothing used by an offshore oil rig company.

Med students who are trying to scrape together enough money to cover their monthly bills can be talked into doing just about anything for a few bucks—even if it involves a wire probe up the bung to measure bodily core temperature to ensure that said student is pulled out of frigid water just before a fatal cardiac arrhythmia ensues.

I ended up doing all three of the designated experiments on the same weekend, spending several hours in a tank of water between freezing and forty degrees. One experiment involved wearing the full oil rig suit, one wearing just the oil rig jacket, and the last wearing just my street clothes. For this act of heroism I was awarded a sack of hamburgers, enough money to cover my car insurance bill, and a fuzzy picture of me in the tank on the front page of the Duluth newspaper. Whoop-de-freakin'-do!

Other than that memorable experience, I absolutely loved the place. By the time we left, we had all done live-in preceptorships with community docs and had observed first-hand how caring physicians really practice. We also had a great group of professors, and many interacted with us socially as well as academically. A number of them were also runners, and a bunch of us kept in shape by running a regular route along Skyline Drive, which had incredible views of Lake Superior. Those who we interacted with only on an academic basis were still extremely engaging, and most were pretty damn funny, sometimes without even trying.

We were taught clinical medicine by Dr. Pete Bolton, who in a pretty straightforward way presented to us the procedure and process of taking a medical history and doing a physical exam. As green medical students, the process seemed pretty daunting, as the physical and especially the history, when done in their absolute entirety, included an enormous amount of detail. One day Bolton was plodding through the medical history, and he eventually came to the sexuality questions. He related to us the need to ask all of the pertinent questions, and the need to remain professional when given any kind of answer. Citing his personal experience, he recalled asking a young lady the standard question: "Are you sexually active?"

She stared back at him, rolled her eyes, gave him a Valley Girl sigh, and responded, "Well, I don't just lay there."

It was indeed clouding up as I proceeded further north. I wondered if this was a metaphor for everyone's spirits at camp, given the test they'd been through. My own tests were about to begin as well . . .

Chapter 11

I arrived back at camp to find the weather there as gloomy as everyone's mood. Schmitty, true to his word as always, had procured the cherry picker, which was parked in along the jack pines at the end of the driveway. It was so foggy, I damn near caught the edge of the thing as I was making the turn onto the gravel driveway. I worked my way through the thick cloud of fog up to the open garage. The crew was hanging around, beers in hand, quieter than I think I'd ever seen them.

"God, I'm glad to see that you are all okay," I breathed. "What the hell happened?" I added.

"We have no idea," observed Schmitty. "We got a chance to take a look at the woods before this pea soup of a fog set in, and it looks like the fire burned through the woods and into the ravine. The creek there eventually stopped it before it kept burning up toward the cabin. The lake stopped it on the other side, and the wide gravel driveway stopped it on the near side. The old logging road turns into the woods near the far end, and somehow that must have slowed it up enough to burn it out on that side as well."

I went to the Mustang, opened the trunk, removed my backpack, and set it down on a table in the garage. "At least *that* was fortunate," I said, as I dished up a bowl of Schmitty's fresh batch of chili from the crockpot. "I wonder if we'll ever know what started it."

"I think we will," said Schmitty. "That woods was a state forest, and I suspect it won't be long at all before a whole regiment of investigators is up here traipsing around trying to figure out just that. I suspect they would be here today if it weren't for the pea soup. Speaking of which, Doc, it's supposed to rain tonight and then clear up tomorrow. By then I expect the regiment will have arrived. If you want to take that cherry picker out we are going to have to do it right now—fog and all."

"What the hell are you two up to?" inquired Gus.

"Doc has a biological interest in the top of a large pine tree," answered Schmitty.

"Nothing any more dangerous than we've done before," I added.

"I'll vouch for that," said Steve.

We left the group at the garage and walked down the long driveway toward the cherry picker. "Any trouble getting hold of that thing?" I asked.

"Naw," came the reply, "he owes me."

"I won't ask."

"Don't."

We arrived, fog unrelenting, at the end of the driveway. "You know how to run this thing?" I asked.

"It's got a motor, a steering wheel, and a couple of levers," came the reply. "Fred Flintstone could do it."

"Yeah, but could Fred do it in a fog like this?"

"Fred could do anything. Speaking of which, you've answered the Ginger or Mary Ann question for me, but you keep avoiding the Betty or Wilma question."

"Fantasizing about cartoon characters seems just a bit weird to me, man. But Wilma, definitely Wilma. I also thought Veronica had—"

"All right!" he interrupted me. "Now you're starting to weird *me* out."

By then Schmitty had swung up onto the seat of the cherry picker and was spinning the engine over. The thing coughed and sputtered loudly, probably from a combination of age, inactivity, and humidity.

Eventually it started to fire, and with a little tweaking of the choke and the throttle, began to idle smoothly. "Pull up the coordinates, Doc, and let's get this show on the road."

I pulled up the information on the phone, and we headed down the old logging road toward what used to be the far edge of the woods. A few breaks in the fog gave me a sickening view of the devastation that the fire had wreaked. We both shook our heads and motored on to the end of the logging road, where it turned in toward the woods.

"We're getting close," I announced. "I'd say up another fifty feet or so, and then we have to turn into the woods, or what used to be the woods."

"There is a clump of trees back in behind the area where we are turning in that didn't burn down. I noticed them when we looked around this morning. I really don't know why they're still standing," Schmitty drawled.

As we turned the cherry picker into the woods, I began, per my plan, to think about *Joy*. Not knowing her name, I had decided to assign her one, and Joy seemed appropriate. I suspected now, going back into the vortex, that I could potentially use its power for any number of purposes, depending on the thoughts that I chose to occupy my mind while within it. The ethical implications of any such action were complex, but the only purpose of my return was to find Joy.

We rolled up to the exact spot of the coordinates on my phone and stopped. Schmitty shut the cherry picker down. There was dead silence. "I feel like I'm on the set of *The Hound of the Baskervilles*," I said as I peered into the dense fog.

"What's the plan?" said Schmitty. "I know why you wanted to come back here, and it sounds like she's worth it."

"I can't even begin to describe her," I said—but I went ahead and did so anyway, recounting to Schmitty the exact details of those three minutes at the Jug and exactly what she looked like. Not knowing her name, I told him the one I had given her.

"I hope if we get you back into that vortex while you're thinking of her, that you'll see something or realize something that will help you find her. But if we do get you back up into that thing, I don't know how long you'll need to be up there."

"I don't know either," I answered.

"I also don't know how long we have before it starts to

rain heavily, which might make it impossible for us to drive this thing back out of here," he said.

"We'll just have to do what we can," I replied, "but there is one thing I want to quickly try before you send me up in that thing."

"What's that?"

"I want to send *you* up in that thing."

"What, and if I survive, then you'll go up?"

"No, I just want to see if you experience anything when I put you in the vortex. I want to know what this thing is—if it is something that anyone can experience, or something that only I can experience. You don't have to be up there for long—I suspect you'll know right away if you are experiencing anything like I did."

"I'm up for that," he said, "but let's get to it."

We fired up the engine again, and Schmitty showed me how to run the controls. He climbed into the basket, and I slowly raised him up within the coordinate point. It was way too noisy to communicate by yelling, and the fog was making it difficult to see.

The heat of the engine must have started to clear some of the fog near the basket, because I suddenly could see Schmitty looking down at me as he lifted his arms, palms upward, suggesting to me that nothing was happening. I pointed left and then pointed right, suggesting that he move around in the basket, which he did. I then tipped my head back and pointed backward with my fingers to get him to do the same. He did, tipping his head back while moving around in the basket. He again gave me the palms-up sign. As I sat there trying to figure out what to do, I noticed that he kept moving his arms and pointing down toward the ground. I assumed that that was the signal for me to lower him, which I did. He climbed out of the basket and came over to me and said, "Nothin'. Your turn, Doc."

I climbed into the basket, and Schmitty slowly raised me up above the coordinate point—foggy again—to the estimated height where I remembered the tree stand was. I waited a few moments and felt absolutely nothing. I kept Joy and nothing else on my mind, other than being open to the presence of the vortex. Moving around inside the basket, I still sensed nothing. By then I started thinking about having Schmitty raise or lower the basket a few feet in case my height estimate was off. The rain had started to come down, which began clearing the fog, and I tipped my head back to look up.

Instantly, I was back in the vortex. The familiar feelings came rushing back as I began to float in the blue-green cloud. My head started to expand as the feelings of tranquility and warmth overtook me. "Spill the Wine" was playing in the background. This time, everything seemed to happen almost in an instant as I opened myself up to what I knew was coming.

As I floated on, I could see the cloud begin to separate and an image begin to form. As it came into focus, I could sense a familiarity with its outlines. It was a city, a city that I began to recognize. The buildings looked vaguely familiar, yet completely familiar—but I still couldn't identify them. Then a zoom down onto a street, a street that was lined with older, yet very well-maintained buildings. A woman was walking down the street, and the image began to focus in on her . . .

A loud bang knocked me right out of the vortex—with a sudden surge replaced quickly by a sensation of extreme heaviness.

Dammit, I thought, *I was so close . . .*

Chapter 12

My first thought was that the engine in the old beast of a cherry picker had backfired. When the second bang presented an instantaneous ricochet off of the lower extension arm of the basket, it was obvious that I was dealing with a combustion problem—but not one involving gasoline. As I quickly dropped down inside the enclosed basket, a third shot rang out. This one, however, didn't come from the edge of the charred woods, as the first two apparently had. It seemed to come from . . . below? The confusion quickly cleared as the engine shut down and I heard a groan from the woods' edge—and remembered who and what was below me. Schmitty, packing as ever, had fired the third shot.

"You okay, Doc?" I heard from below.

"Yeah," I yelled. I wasn't hit, and I wasn't bleeding, and I felt very little of the heaviness that I felt the last time I had exited the vortex.

I heard the engine start and felt the basket dropping quickly as Schmitty pulled me out of the air and back to the ground. "Stay in the basket," he yelled. He had killed the engine and snuck along the extension arm, using the basket as cover. I saw an arm come over the near edge of the basket, handing me a loaded Beretta nine millimeter.

I raised my voice just enough for him to hear me and said, "Why are you giving me your gun?"

"That's *your* gun," he replied. "If you can bring one piece, why not bring two? I'll cover you while you crawl out the back, and then we're going to slink toward the woods and flush out the son of a bitch that's interrupting our party."

I crawled out the back of the basket and dropped to the ground. I looked at Schmitty. "Thanks, man," I said in a low voice.

"What are friends for if they can't come packin' in a time of need?" he laughed.

"I think you hit him," I said.

"I know I hit him," he replied. "Didn't you hear the groan?"

"Yes I did, but let's still be careful."

We slowly and carefully made our way to the remaining edge of the woods, weapons drawn. From our contact point with the woods, we searched about fifty feet back toward the direction of the logging road, and then started in the other direction. About twenty-five feet in that direction, I motioned to Schmitty. "Here's where he was," I said.

We both looked down at a spot where two spent rifle cartridges lay, next to a small spot of blood. We fanned out in several directions, trying to locate a blood trail, but the rain was making it impossible to continue. At least it had cleared out the fog. We looked at each other and decided to give up the search.

"What the hell was that about?" Schmitty growled. "Far as I know, my ex-wife doesn't own a gun, and the IRS hasn't started hiring hit men."

"I don't think those shots were meant for you, buddy, and I'm equally confused and equally pissed. I don't have an ex-wife, and I also have no freakin' idea of anyone in particular who might want to phlebotomize me by way of bullet." At that point, I still didn't have enough information about my blowout to foster further speculation, and the fuzzy details from the end of my first trip into the vortex didn't really add anything either.

"All I know," quipped Schmitty, "is that it's getting weirder around here by the minute. First, your *vortex* thing, then the woods fire, and now we're a couple of ducks in a shooting gallery. None of this shit makes any sense. You sure you haven't pissed anyone off, Doc?"

"In the ER, it's always possible, but not that I'm aware of—lately, anyway. There are always druggies who don't get what they want, but they typically just move on to another doctor." *Of course*, I thought to myself, *there could be a few* Jimmys *out there . . .*

"Well," Schmitty proclaimed, "you're going to have to rack your brain and see if there is a he or a *she* you can come up with—because Doc, for once, you're right. Those bullets had *your* name on them."

Chapter 13

By then, the rain was starting to come down in sheets. We sloshed our way back out of the small patch of remaining woods and made it back to the cherry picker. My rubber boots were already making sucking sounds as I extricated them from the muck.

"If we don't get this thing out of here right now," Schmitty said, "we'll bury it up to the axles when we try to move it. By the way," he added, "thanks for the $500 you sent me last year."

"What are you talking about?" I replied.

"Shut the hell up—you know what I'm talking about," came the retort.

Before I could ask if he was sure nothing happened when he was in the vortex, he had swung his way up onto the seat of the cherry picker. "Jump on," he said. "I'm gonna gun the hell out of this thing."

With Schmitty being a man of his word, the next few minutes resembled a monster truck race in a mud hole. We dug, and spun, and twisted, and laughed our asses off. We probably could have gotten the damn thing back to the road a little easier, but the unspoken sheer relief of being alive and the craziness of the entire situation brought out a repressed sandbox mentality in both of us.

We eventually managed to spin out of the burnt-out

woods and back onto the logging trail. Schmitty reached over, opened the toolbox of the cherry picker, and produced two beers. I laughed so hard that I almost fell off of the fender that I was sitting on.

"The guns, that was *prepared*," I said. "This," I added, "is *really prepared*."

We rolled along the old logging road toward the gravel driveway leading back to the cabin. The rain was letting up a bit by that time, and I could see the outline of a man at the end of the logging road, standing next to what looked like an old two-ton truck hooked to a trailer.

"That's Diggie," yelled Schmitty over the roar of the engine.

We progressed on to the end of the logging road and rolled the cherry picker up to the back of the trailer.

"Howdy boys," said a voice that was low and growling but yet somehow cheerful at the same time.

"How's the bar business, my man?" said Schmitty.

"One day at a time," came the response. "I tried to call you, Schmitty, but got no answer—probably because this old beast is so loud you couldn't hear it. I was trying to let you know that this thing does not do well at all on muddy terrain, and when the rain started pouring . . ."

"We found that out," Schmitty laughed, "and just in the nick of time. You know, Diggie, given that the feds almost certainly will be here tomorrow to investigate the fire, it's probably best that you take the beast back with you tonight—less questions that way if they see it and wonder what the hell we were doing with it. A couple more hours of rain, and other than maybe some leftover tracks in the woods, there'll be little if any evidence that this thing was ever here."

"Gotcha, man," he said, and with that we loaded the cherry picker onto the trailer and watched Diggie drive away.

"He didn't ask any questions either," I said.

"Nope," came the reply.

By that time we were absolutely soaking wet and standing at the edge of the gravel driveway. Schmitty pulled out two more beers, one from each pocket, and handed one to me as we began walking back to the cabin.

"No doubt those guys heard the gunshots," I said. "What are we going to tell them?"

"For now, we tell them we were shooting at crows," Schmitty said. "You, Doc, are the one who needs to be careful. We don't know who this is, why he is trying to ventilate your hide, or if he is still a threat. I could have hit him in the arm, or in the chest—no idea, but he's likely gone from here, at least for the time being."

We walked back into camp, loudly discussing the finer points of pine tree architecture.

Chapter 14

The rain let up gradually, and finally stopped at about 8 p.m. It was relatively cool outside, but when the sky cleared, that didn't seem to matter. We were all in the mood for a nice roaring fire, and I was in the mood for a little more than that. I finished up another bowl of chili and mixed up a rum and Coke.

By that time, I was more than a little pissed at myself, because I had reached to pull out my phone a few minutes earlier to check the weather report and realized that it was missing. I had searched around camp and walked back along the gravel driveway to where the cherry picker had been parked and had been unable to find it. By then, it was getting too dark to look any further, and I wanted a drink.

I realize I'm somewhat of a control freak—and the fear of losing control (among other reasons) is why I avoid drugs and generally try to avoid drinking too much. (Fortunately for me, I also usually get sleepy after about two beers.) After the events of the day, however, control wasn't on the top of my list. Schmitty and I were both aware that there was more to discuss about our experience with the cherry picker, but it seemed that we both needed to loosen up a bit before we were ready to embark on that journey. I had already told him that I thought I'd made it back into the vortex, but I wasn't sure exactly what I'd seen.

The first order of business was dinner, and Steve had brought up two huge trays of a tater-tot hot dish (how Minnesotan is that?) that tasted so good it drove me to remark, "Someone should marry that man!"

"You already did, don't you remember?" he said. "I'm absolutely crushed that you don't remember our ceremony," he added.

"I'll *never* forget the Bahamas," I said with a wink.

Steve and his wife had decided to take a vacation in the Bahamas, and out of curiosity I had peppered them for details, having never been there myself. I think they finally got so tired of my questions that they suggested that I just go along, which I did. After moving here from Chicago, Steve had not had a lot of time to develop new friends before we met in the church choir. We had hit it off and started hanging out together, going fishing, playing music together, and the like. Ann's family eventually decided that I was Steve's wife, or Steve was my wife—didn't matter, they were just having fun with it. We decided to make it official in the Bahamas when we, walking along the beach, came across a little gazebo that had recently been decked out for a wedding. We held hands, and Ann took pictures for the family back home. About that time two elderly women from New York walked by and sighed, "Isn't that sweet!" We tried to explain that the lady taking pictures was Steve's wife, but they would have nothing of it. "It's okay, boys," they remarked, and continued walking down the beach. They were right.

We polished off both trays of the tater-tot hot dish and headed down to the fire, drinks in hand. Schmitty had the nine millimeter strapped to his belt.

"So, what world problems are we going to solve tonight?" asked Steve.

"Personally," said Dan, "I am extremely concerned about our southern border crisis."

"And I'm sure that you have a proposed solution," replied Steve.

"Of course I do," responded Dan. "*All* Iowans—each and every one of them—are only allowed to cross into Minnesota if they have a valid short stay visa."

I looked over at Steve, who just sat there and shook his head.

"No guitars tonight, fellas?" asked Gus.

"After the other night, we thought we'd give you a rest," I replied.

"Don't do that on my account," offered Gus. "I thoroughly enjoyed the serenade."

"Say," Gus continued, "Schmitty was telling me about the copyright battle you are having with one of the songs on your album. What happened?"

"I wish I knew exactly myself," I said.

I went on to explain the story of playing the song at the Jug Lounge the night before I sent the material on the album in for copyright. Several weeks later I was still waiting for confirmation of my copyright, so I finally decided to contact the Library of Congress directly.

"I bet that went smooth as silk," Gus chuckled.

"*Sure* it did," I muttered. "I realize that the place is huge and that copyrights run in the millions, but the phone tree I had to crawl through there was unbelievable."

I explained that copyright registration itself does not establish the submitter's ownership of the material being copyrighted. The rights protected by copyright actually come into existence even earlier, when the artist or author places the substantially completed work in a tangible form. The submission of material—and the formal "granting" of a copyright—acts merely as a time-stamp recognition of created material for purposes of any future legal action. Whoever has the material on file first is presumptively treated as the owner of the material.

After that, if someone's later submitted material reads or sounds like someone else's previously submitted material, then an act of infringement may have occurred. Practically speaking, this only happens when a piece of material has been successfully sold and another later successful piece of material is deemed by the original submitter to have infringed upon his or her work. The classic example in the world of music is "He's So Fine" by the Chiffons in the early 1960s, followed later by "My Sweet Lord" by George Harrison.

The copyright office itself cannot, and does not, make it a habit to listen to or read every piece of material submitted to it to make a judgment if that material is indeed "new." That would be impossible. It is up to individuals to make a claim that their work has been infringed upon, if indeed they believe that has happened.

"What happened in my case," I went on, "was decidedly unusual. Individuals can submit a copyright online, or through the mail. The day after I sang 'Love Story' at the Jug, I dropped the packet for the copyright of the album, which included that song, in the mail. Unbeknownst to me, apparently someone else also submitted a copyright—word for word and note for note—for 'Love Story' the same day. I can only assume that someone recorded the song at the Jug that night and quickly put together a submission. What I finally found out, after making it through the phone tree, was that both submissions had landed on the same person's desk *on the same day*—a practical impossibility, but it nonetheless occurred."

"What happened then?" asked Gus.

"Not much of anything for a while," I said. "I waited it out, and as they were trying to figure out what to do with it, I heard through the grapevine that Allied Sound Group, a regional recording concern, had signed an artist to do a song called 'Our Love Story (Is Ours Alone).'"

"*Your* song," said Schmitty.

"Word for word—note for note, as it turned out," I said.

"So what did you do?" asked Gus.

"First, I called the guy who stole my song."

"And?"

"He suggested I do something that was anatomically impossible."

"Then what?"

"I got an attorney," I answered. "Just like every other American, I'm not a fan of lawyers or doctors unless I need one myself. In this case, I needed one, and the whole thing is still at a stalemate."

"Do you think they'll ever get it figured out?" asked Steve.

"Eventually, I suppose. My attorney asked me if anyone could witness that we had played the song at the Jug that night from sheet music or lead sheets. Much better than that would have been a video recording of me doing the song that night. Unfortunately, Alex has passed on, and the other two guys who played with us back then—before we re-formed the band—moved out of state, and despite my attempts, I've never been able to make contact with them. The re-formed band eventually recorded the entire album, including that song, but I've held off on releasing it until this issue is settled."

The sky was absolutely clear and the celestial globe was beautiful and bright—so much brighter here than around the Twin Cities. This was the perfect spot to catch a glimpse of the aurora borealis, better known as the northern lights, which were rumored to be making an appearance later that night.

I brought up the subject and was regaled by Dan—the Cliff Clavin of fishing camp—about the origin of their name. Apparently this one was a double shot of mythology, combining Aurora—the Roman goddess of dawn—

with Boreas, the Greek name for the north wind. "Cliff" proceeded further to inform us—in *Fargo* fashion—that the only other two mythological gods ever connected with Minnesota were "Casserolius" and his Greek counterpart, "Hotdyshius." At that point, four of us proceeded to lift him—chair and all—and were preparing to toss him into the fire. Something grabbed hold of us—ethics, or thirst, or more likely the realization that we could never explain this one to the cops—and we put him back down.

Looking at the sky, I thought of my last trip to the Nobel Conference with Mark Lansing: a mind-blowing experience, really. The conference was about the limits of the universe, and the discussions, as always, ran from the scientific to the theistic.

I looked up. "Do you know how many stars are actually out there?" I said.

"Not exactly," said Dan, "but something tells me I'm about to find out."

I told them about the Nobel Conference and the remarkable lecture presentations Mark and I had attended. "So, my understanding is that our universe is around 13.8 billion years old, constantly expanding, and contains ten *to the twenty-second power* stars—ten followed by twenty-two zeroes," I said. "As to the incredible expanse of the universe, apparently there are around one hundred billion galaxies in the universe, but we can only see about one hundred of them. To top that off, galaxies make up only 5 percent of the total space of the universe. In our Milky Way galaxy alone, there are something like four hundred billion stars, and it is one hundred light-years across just that one galaxy.

"I'd also heard this fact before," I added, "but the light from the typical star we see is actually somewhere between one hundred and one thousand years old, which absolutely fascinates me."

"All of which can either make you feel small and insignificant," said Mike, "or drive your narcissism if you feel—like some apparently do—that despite all of that vast expanse, we here on Earth are the only living beings in the universe."

I sipped my beer and thought about that for a bit, realizing that it was raising the whole predestination debate in my brain again. In fact, in thinking about why I didn't turn around that night at the Jug Lounge, I at one point had surprisingly, but briefly, studied the concept of astral projection as a way to help come to grips with deciding whether I myself had made the decision, or if the decision was somehow made for me. Often, wondering why I had ended up in medicine instead of fully pursuing music usually ended up sparking the same internal debate. Even being the skeptic I am, I found the whole concept of astral travel quite intriguing. My reading about the makeup of the astral world had led me to note that those who had claimed to have been there had many different ideas about the concept—though most seemed to believe that seven levels existed, from the Earth plane up to the highest plane of enlightenment.

I shared my thoughts about predestination with Mike.

"You know," he said, "I've thought about that too, and I

keep coming back to one blunt realization. It's pretty damn hard for me to believe in the concept of free will when I keep reading about the arrests of fourteen-year-old crack whores in East Saint Louis."

"I suppose it is possible—in this vast universe—that you choose some things, and that ultimately, some things are chosen *for* you," said Dan.

"Whatever the case," I answered, "if the explosion of stars gave us the heavy elements in our bodies, we certainly share something with the universe. To quote Carl Sagan: 'We are star stuff.'"

Chapter 15

I was planning on visiting my college professors the next day to discuss their communication with me, and I really wanted to hear what the guys at camp thought about the categories my profs had laid out for me. Thus began an incredibly interesting dialogue that, as far as I was concerned, could have run the whole night if we all didn't eventually need to get some sleep. My thoughts from my two visits to the vortex were flooding my brain, including sharp and clear thoughts about emotion and human interaction. I knew that Schmitty, especially, would have strong feelings about what we were about to discuss, and I welcomed his opinion. Given my time in the vortex, I was anxious to see how I myself would react to the discussion.

"After you talk to your college profs about this, we need to have another discussion, because I'd really like to hear what they had to say," said Schmitty. "I suspect they will have a slightly different take on these issues than we do, but it's obvious that we'll never make any headway if both sides don't at least agree to respect each other's right to an opinion."

"So," I said to Schmitty, "you were one of Father Dean's altar boys too, and I'm sure you remember his famous 'Fall of the Roman Empire' sermon."

"Indeed I do," Schmitty answered.

"Well," I said, "it came roaring back to me as soon as I saw the response from my college profs that I showed you guys the other night. I found myself suddenly back in a sociology class at Saint John's discussing societal theory relating to how societies survive over time by maintaining internal stability. As I recall, in primitive nonsociologically advanced groups, everyone was expected to perform the similar tasks that were necessary for survival. As societies advanced, their members began to perform fundamentally different tasks that, over time, advanced their knowledge—as well as their cultural, economic, and social well-being.

"Inherent in this, though," I continued, "especially as societies grew, was the further separation of individuals from each other, and the resultant strain on the equilibrium of their society based on an ever-changing definition of exactly what function that society was supposed to perform."

"Enter organized government," said Gus.

"Exactly," I said. "But, as societies advanced and became more affluent—including our own—their governments' ideas of what a society was expected to do for itself, and for its individuals, increased exponentially as those individuals became further separated from each other."

"And," said Gus, "as government became further separated from the people."

"Bingo," I said, "which begs the debate of point number one: Individual Responsibility vis-à-vis The Role of Big Government."

"I'll weigh in on that one," offered Schmitty. "My

problem with big government is that you get results similar to sending someone to an all-you-can-eat buffet, where the consumption can be massive. We live in a fantastic country—one where we have continuously fought for the freedom to pursue life as we so choose. *As we so choose*, however, are the operative words here. What we have fought for is the equal *opportunity* to live life as we so choose, not the guarantee of *equality* in its outcome—as promised by big government or anyone else. That was the basis of Martin Luther King's argument. The beauty of living in America today is that the circumstances of your birth don't necessarily determine the circumstances of your life, and this remains true as long as we preserve equal opportunity. Multitudes of people are scratching to get to capitalist America for exactly that reason. It's much easier to get from nothing to something here than it is anywhere else in the world."

"I've been around a lot longer than any of you guys, and I'll vouch for that being true," interjected Gus.

"Having equal opportunity," Schmitty continued, "still means that people make their own choices, and as such, income inequality will automatically exist. Unfortunately, politicians who use class warfare as a political tool will also automatically exist—and will be at the ready to cast you the rescue net once they have established your victimhood.

"The efforts of government toward creating equal outcomes for everyone," he finished, "only serve to denigrate the preservation of equal opportunity. Government's role should be to help guarantee the opportunity and then get the hell out of the way—to help keep the playing field level, but not be in charge of running the plays. Respecting each other's differences may mean respecting the level of effort that certain individuals are willing to put forth. It also means respecting the efforts of highly motivated individuals who built this country, and the similar effort that will be necessary for its continued growth and existence. In the end, government redistribution of income does not level the playing field—it sinks it. We need to get to a place where government departments stop measuring their success by the size of their budgets—meaning that just because society has discovered a problem doesn't mean it's government's job to fix it."

"It's interesting that literary dystopian societies," responded Dan, "are usually based on conformity and social control, typically imposed by an oppressive bureaucracy. My fear, to paraphrase Jefferson, is that a government big enough to give you everything is also big enough to take it away."

"That kind of sums it up," said Mike.

"Maybe, but that brings up another point," added Schmitty. "Personally, I don't have a stake in how individually successful any one person chooses to become or not become—or how they choose to live their life—and I'm always willing to offer help to anyone who genuinely needs it. If I do help, however, I want to reserve the right—if you are standing neck deep in shit—to ask how you got there, because maybe I can offer some advice as well as opening my checkbook. As it stands now, when it comes to taxes, I'm expected to just pay up and shut up—which means that I might be working extra hours to help pay for your eighth trip through rehab instead of being able to add to my son's college fund. Where's the fairness in that for me? Yes, I know someone will tell me that someday I may need help too, which may be true, but I'm tired of being expected to just fork it over and not ask any questions. I realize that society changes over time, but its best interests aren't always the ones being driven, or the ones we can afford to keep paying for."

"Which, I guess, could bring us to point number two: Passing Judgment vis-à-vis Societal Expectations," I said.

"I have a comment on that, too," said Schmitty.

"Shocking," offered Steve.

Schmitty shot him a look and continued, "I pride myself on being a pretty good observer of human behavior. I've seen plenty of people pack their bags, buy the roadmap, gas up the car, and drive—with full intent—straight to Crapville. They arrive in town and look around for a while, do some shopping, and eventually decide they hate the surroundings. By then, the car is out of gas, and society gets tapped to fill the tank to get the car back out of town. I, as a member of society, am expected to foot part of that bill while being simultaneously told how *privileged* I am to be able to work to do it. I really don't mind paying taxes. I just don't like to see my money wasted.

"But, we are not heartless," he continued, "and emotionally we reach out to these people. *Realistically*, we should be impressing upon them that it is they themselves who ultimately need to figure out how to exit town, because the city is getting so big that we can't afford to keep depopulating it. Instead, once they've arrived, we don't ask questions. We don't allow them just one wrong turn—or one rehab stint or one teenage pregnancy—but instead keep paying for repeated bad driving habits, supported by massive taxation. Do we ever draw the line on anything? Americans apparently now spend more on taxes than on all their basic needs, despite the fact that the top 10 percent of income earners now pay about 70 percent of all federal taxes. I just heard that around half of every tax dollar we currently spend goes to entitlements, and that we still *borrow* a big chunk of every dollar we spend—at one point it was as high as forty cents. Government appears ready to spend whatever it can get its hands on."

"Just because government *can* provide something doesn't necessarily mean it *should*," offered Steve.

"Agreed," Schmitty added. "We seem to have some weird twist on Marxism going on, where we give to everyone according to the government's perception of their need—even if it's self-imposed—while we don't demand that many in that same group produce according to their ability. We all started out with the right to life, liberty, and the pursuit of happiness—not a job, health care, and housing. Our future economic security is based on each generation doing better than the next, and it looks to me like we're headed in the wrong direction. That, Doc, is the downhill spiral Father Dean was talking about, and the closing frames of that movie aren't a happy ending. Rome is burning, and we're fiddling away micromanaging the small stuff."

"I do think that's the message he was trying to get across," I added.

"Do I get to pass judgment?" Schmitty pressed on. "I won't judge you in the least for what you do, as long as it doesn't hurt me or my family, and as long as I and/or society don't have to pay for it. If that does happen, though, you have invited me into your world, and all bets are off. However, if we really are all in this together, then I believe there should be responsibility at *every* level. If anyone chooses to complain about a lack of jobs for working-class America, then they should also be willing to own two $300 American-made TVs instead of four $150 imported ones. In the end, I have faith in people, and when they *really* need to jump in and get the job done, most will respond. If, however, we disincent them to respond, or constantly tell them that they can't overcome the same types of obstacles that other people face, that may not happen."

"So, at this point, how do you get your message across without being skewered?" asked Jake.

"Exactly," echoed Dustin. "I can imagine how far this conversation would run on a lot of college campuses before someone would render that their opinion is the only one that matters by vilifying yours, instead of opening up a dialogue. I've seen the hypocrisy in action. Some demand the unlimited freedom to do what they want, when they want—

while simultaneously acting as the sole arbiter of what's *offensive* when other people do what *they* want. Others loudly, and correctly, proclaim that no one should denigrate an entire group based on the actions of a few, then simultaneously label the entire opposing political party as a bunch of 'blithering idiots,' and all men on campus as 'potential rapists.'"

"Now we're getting somewhere," I said excitedly. "Why should this type of behavior exist at places that are supposedly institutions of higher learning—places where people should be championing the ideal of freedom of thought?"

"Political correctness," observed Steve.

"Yes!" I exclaimed. "The heart of the matter, and I suspect the place where my profs were leading me with point number three: The Dialogue of Conflict vis-à-vis Political Correctness."

"We see this all the time at school," said Dustin. "There may be somewhat of a generational component to it, as we have been so programmed to avoid conflict, and you really cannot have a productive dialogue that way. It seems now that the first step with any really charged issue is not how to debate the issue, but how to discredit the person on the other side—which also seems to be the modus operandi of a large number of politicians these days, and, I think, the reason why people are so polarized. The unfortunate offshoot of extreme polarization is that, in the end, nothing of any meaning gets accomplished. It should be obvious that no one ever gets everything they want, but there are plenty of people out there still pushing the envelope.

"As for politicians, when the number-one priority at any

point in your term is re-election instead of concentrating on what you were actually elected for, this type of behavior isn't a big surprise—but it sure is a big problem. No matter how it comes off, the real intent is an attempt at suppressing speech, often using some sort of political correctness fallback position to support it—and people out there are literally tripping over each other to capture the PC sweepstakes."

"I couldn't agree more on the PC issue," Jake said. "At school, it seems like we are literally being taught how to be offended, so we can then tie on the Social Justice Hero cape and save the world from the effects of deadly evils like cultural misappropriation. Last year, I thought, *screw it*," he added. "I decided to dress like myself for Halloween—I mean, the *Autumn Festival*—and I challenged anyone to find a way to take offense."

"And?" Dustin asked.

"Someone accused me of failing to embrace diversity."

Dustin shook his head. "We all understand the need for appropriate cultural sensitivity," he said, "but some of this is just ridiculous."

"So, how did we end up at this point?" I asked.

"I've thought about that extensively," said Dustin, "and the only explanation I have that seems to make any sense is guilt—pure and simple guilt. My friends and I talk about this all the time. We have been educated to feel guilty about just about everything. There's *wealth* guilt, and *gender* guilt, and *race* guilt, and *American* guilt, and several others—all built on the foundation of political correctness. The implicit message from these 'lovers of freedom' is: toe the line or you'll get reminded how awful you really are just because you exist. The irony is that silencing your critics is a commonplace tactic in authoritarian countries."

"I was thinking about the exact same thing during a class the other day," said Jake, "when this smug-looking freshman tried to pull the same crap on a girl who voiced an opinion about an issue that came out slightly off of college mainstream."

"What happened?" I asked.

"I looked him square in the eye and reminded him that the suppression of free speech in Hitler's Germany was inextricably tied to the Holocaust."

"Way to go!" said Schmitty.

"Made me feel a lot better," said Jake, "and so did she, later that night!"

Dustin pushed him off his chair as the group verbally antagonized him.

"I know that guy. Isn't he in pre-med?" Dustin asked Jake, as Jake picked himself up off the ground.

"The only way that guy is going to get into medical school is as a cadaver," came the reply.

The fire was dying down as Dustin and Jake went to the woodshed and came back with a wheelbarrow full of cut pine. It snapped and popped as it was strategically added to the flames, sending hundreds of mini embers skyward. The night was cooling off rapidly, and the added warmth was welcome.

"You're deep in thought over there, Doc," said Gus. "Where do you weigh in on all of this politically?"

I took a deep breath. "I'm a guy who really doesn't like to mince words," I answered, "but I'm always careful when someone asks me that question—for two reasons. The first is that inevitably, someone will try to tie you into a particular political persuasion, and the second is that I regard anything that I say as merely my opinion and nothing more—except perhaps a starting point for discussion.

"Call me what you will," I added, "but I consider myself to be socially progressive and fiscally responsible—which probably defies any sort of labeling anyway. My biggest concern is where society is headed. I see it in things as simple as the cultural shift from the statement 'I deserve' instead of 'I earned.'"

"That's Father Dean coming through again," said Schmitty.

"Probably," I answered, "but overall, I think reasonable people *and* both major political parties want the same thing—which is for all people to have the chance to lead happy and productive lives. The big question is: What is government's role—if any—in getting us there? Conservatives lament that liberals just want to spend money now and ask questions later, and liberals point out that they do it for good reasons. Liberals lament that conservatives just want to end social programs, and conservatives point out that if that were true, they would have done it when they were in power. Unfortunately, the debate seems to end right there. I don't know if it's just the point we have evolved to, or if it is some offshoot of our sound-bite culture, but Dustin is right—just beyond this point, labels get assigned and the vilification begins. We need to hear consistent opinions from both sides of any issue to start a proper debate and arrive at a reasonable consensus.

"Individuals also tend to bring their own context when it comes to any subject. For example, in debating gender issues, I, as a physician, might go straight to the biological, whereas someone else might go to the socio-cultural. The acceptance of individual context increases the likelihood that productive debate will continue. As has been said, true tolerance is owing the other side at least the presumption of good faith, which includes honestly listening to their entire position. It also includes, when necessary, the ability to accept basic common-sense principles over ideological ones."

"My point exactly," said Dustin.

"You would think," I continued, "that we all could find one good starting point to agree on that would cement the commencement of an effective national debate, but vilification seems to be more effective as a tool for political power, so why bother even beginning a debate on what really matters? If we can't all agree on a starting point—for example, Schmitty's point about the craziness at the federal level of borrowing a large amount of what we currently spend—then we are doomed. One side ends up getting vilified for concentrating on the big picture, and the other for concentrating on the small picture—which means we don't come up with a decent picture of anything at all—and somehow the hypocrisy associated with all of this *tolerance* goes unrecognized."

"Usually, one side seems to get painted by the actions

of its extremists," offered Jake.

"I do agree that extremism on either end never does anyone any good," I said. "Beyond that, the problem I have with the left is that they put too much pressure on big government to solve social issues. The problem I have with the right is that they put too much pressure on big government to solve social issues. I'm for the party that concentrates on the true role of federal government—liberty, and national and economic security—but I'm not holding my breath.

"I'd like to see everyone do as well as they possibly can," I said, "but in all things I try to keep the bigger picture in mind. If you can grasp the bigger picture you can then start to focus on the smaller details that are actually important, instead of getting mired in the ones that aren't. In medicine, even when dealing with individuals we have to apply bigger picture thinking, and a lot of what I see in medicine relates to what I see in society, which is why I like to use it as a comparison.

"In medicine, as in society, the more we do *for* people, the less they seem to do for themselves. People seem to hate to be reminded that we really are just higher-order animals, and as such, we still harbor behaviors that mimic those of the animal kingdom. The more we feed bread to those geese in the park, the less they fend for themselves, and I'm sorry to say that I observe this trait among humans regularly. There are conditions in society that, to some degree, will always exist because society cannot—even in its greatest efforts—override the paths that some individuals choose to take."

"How does this apply to the big picture?" said Schmitty.

"Mainly in how we choose to approach individual situations as they relate to the greater good," I said. "As your car is racing toward the edge of the Grand Canyon, adjusting the seat height may make the ride more comfortable, but applying the brakes more quickly is more likely to result in a better overall outcome.

"We apply small-time thinking to all kinds of situations based on whatever emotion we choose to let rule in that instant, and good long-term policy decisions are generally not emotion based," I added, recalling my revelation in the vortex about the emotion of empathy and the deeper substance of compassion.

"To me, the engagement of compassion is giving a man a fish. The expression of compassion is teaching the man to fish. The fulfillment of compassion—where we hold *everyone's* interests in mind—is eventually requiring him to fish. If we behaved with true compassion, we couldn't face ourselves in the mirror as we collectively pay for those multiple trips through rehab while children in this country aren't fully immunized because of inadequate medical care. True compassion may be telling you early on, as you contemplate living sixty Keith Richards years, that at age fifty-nine you had better start getting your affairs in order, because society is not going to pay to pull your ass out of the fire—opting instead to take care of its children. You can choose to either live a better life, have money put away for the repairs, or be content to check out."

"I bet that idea goes over well with patients," Gus chuckled.

"It's the heresy of all heresies," I answered, "but I, as a physician, truly believe that people should be allowed to behave the way they want—including how much of a healthy lifestyle they choose to maintain. They should then either suffer or enjoy the consequences of that behavior, with the cost of any extraordinary intervention resting solely on their own shoulders—which, to me, cannot be allowed to be painted as the moral equivalent of withholding care. I have come to this conclusion as a result of realizing that the more we try to intervene without putting the true onus on the patient, the less successful we are, and the more money we waste. Until we put people in direct contact with the real cost of medical care as well as with the consequences of their actions, this will never change."

"Now that the government runs more than half of health care, is there any hope that it will ever change?" said Mike.

"Only if they decide to stop micromanaging everything," I said. "As long as we have lifetime politicians, I don't think that will happen. We need people who aren't afraid to be fiscally responsible, and who realize that nothing in society really changes in the long run as a result of just throwing more money at it—and who also realize that society's supply of money for such spending is indeed finite."

"Based on?" said Dan.

"Based on something as simple as the Laffer curve," I said. "Art Laffer was an economist who took a basic idea from other economists, including Keynes, and famously sketched out the concept on a napkin to outline his argument. This happened during the Ford administration in the seventies. The basic argument was that at extreme ends of the tax spectrum, no taxes would be collected. At a tax rate of 0 percent, obviously no tax revenue would be collected, and at a tax rate of 100 percent, no tax revenue would be collected because there would be absolutely no incentive to work. Somewhere in between lies a point where raising taxes further would start to result in falling revenues overall because of the disincentive toward further income earning.

"As to our current situation, a number of experts think we are rapidly approaching that point. Some think a somewhat similar curve can be drawn with self-reliance on one side and entitlement on the other. In that instance, JFK's concept of a rising tide raising all boats doesn't hold water—when some people drill holes in their own boats, and the government drills holes in others. We obviously need major give and take from many quarters if we expect to resolve our issues."

"That's some heavy shit," said Steve, "and on that note, I'm going to hit the rack."

Two hours later, after further discussion, stargazing, and libation, the rest of us reluctantly followed.

I saw Schmitty palm his nine millimeter and sit down in a chair close to the garage. He said he wasn't tired and was going to stay up a while. He didn't fool me a bit.

Chapter 16

I must have been deep in the dream shortly after hitting the pillow, or at least it seemed that way. How else could I have imagined that an experience so vivid and so profound seemed to have happened so quickly? It may have ended vivid and profound, but it certainly didn't start out that way.

My dream started with an overwhelming feeling of despair. I realized that I had gotten into the vortex twice, and I had come so close to seeing what I wanted to see—what I needed to see. Now, I had no tree stand, no tree, no cherry picker, and no phone—which also made me realize that I had no coordinates to even find the right spot again anyway. In the dream, I was sitting in the cabin looking out the window toward where the woods used to be. All I could see, standing shoulder to shoulder in the entire woods, were federal fire investigators—each one holding my phone in their hand.

I closed my eyes, tipped my head down, and cradled it in my hands. Despair surrounded me like a dense fog. Not content to merely surround me, the fog proceeded to stream itself in through my ears and into my brain—like the combined effect of a thousand jackhammers all going off at once. I opened my mouth to scream for help as I lifted my head back up and opened my eyes.

The view outside the cabin had profoundly changed, as had my spirits, which now were intensely calm. Everything was as it had been before the fire, except for a shaft of intense white light that appeared to run from the edge of the cabin, down the driveway, and along the logging road as far as I could see.

I walked over to the cabin door, opened it, and stepped out. Enveloping me completely and immediately was a light so intense that I could see nothing else. Despite its intensity, the light was not blinding or uncomfortable to my eyes. I didn't *feel* any differently, except I soon realized that I was moving. My feet weren't moving, but *I* was moving—enveloped in the shaft of light and proceeding down the driveway, then the logging trail, then into the woods to a familiar tree. I moved upward, still in the shaft of light, until I found myself seated in the tree stand. At that point, the shaft of light disappeared.

Tipping my head back, I found myself again in the swirling blue-green cloud. I waited for the familiar feelings of being in the vortex to begin, but they never did. The more I tried to will myself into the vortex, the more despair set in. Again, I closed my eyes and tipped my head down into my hands. Not knowing who or what I was trying to summon, I implored for help.

When I tilted my head back up and opened my eyes, the shaft of white light had reappeared—next to, but outside of, the tree stand, and even more intense than before. This time it shot straight upward with no end in sight. As I stared at it, a voice that completely surrounded me seemed to breathe, "Step into the light."

Even in a dream, I apparently thought like a doctor. All I could think was: *If you step out beyond this tree stand, the eventual contact with the ground will probably break both of your femurs.* The voice breathed again: "You will not be harmed—step into the light."

I put one foot over the edge, thinking, *At least I know some good orthopedic surgeons*, and followed with the other. As I stepped into the light, I felt an intense and sudden *expansion*. Profound and vivid as it was, it was equally the most calming and soothing experience I could have ever imagined—well beyond even that of the vortex. In fact, it instantly felt like I had attained the maximum tranquility of the vortex, and then moved light-years past it—moving upward in the intense white light. I wanted nothing—absolutely nothing—to ever remove me from the realm that I had entered.

The first realization that I had was that my "existence" had absolutely no boundary—and there is no description for something that is completely devoid of boundary. There was no middle, and there were no edges—no sides, no top, no bottom—no reference points. The closest I can come to explanation is to say that I felt like a pail of water that was being poured out onto an infinite flat surface. I didn't become part of my surroundings—I *was* my surroundings, some sort of cosmic Klein bottle with no orientable surface or boundary.

What am I? was my first thought, as I instantly realized that the answer to the "Who am I?" question held absolutely no meaning for me.

"You are an astral being," came the response to me—not an auditory response, but simply a response of knowing.

Who are you? was my next thought.

"I am your astral guide."

I realized a sudden and intense need for the answer to my inquiry: *What is the vortex?*

"What you call the vortex is the repository of the soul between human habitations," came the response, "when the soul still resides in the lower second plane—the astral plane. Only you and a few others in human history have stumbled into it in a state of alertness and then stayed there long enough to recognize it. You are now likely aware that such an occurrence can—at least transiently—amplify the innate human abilities that occupy your thoughts at that time, and that some of what you envision about your life therein may re-present itself to you in your dreams. To help you understand, I can tell you that others have rapidly passed through their vortex during events such as air travel and were barely aware of the experience, or simply slept through it and thus remained unchanged."

I started to pose a thought question . . .

"I am aware that you have many questions, and I can assist you in finding the answers as we move along our astral journey. With my help, we may move as high as the fourth plane. We may observe, but *together* we are not allowed to enter. I, as an enlightened soul, have recently entered the fourth plane, and therefore I no longer need to experience reincarnation in order to continue my evolution toward the seventh plane."

My thoughts drifted immediately to the obvious: *What is the seventh plane?*

"The plane of the spirit realm," came the response. "At this highest level, souls lose their form and become one with God. This is said to be the domain of the creator, or possibly the sum total of completely purified souls."

Sooo, I inquired, *right now, I am a* soul*?*

"Not completely," came the response. "On this astral journey, you are a soul *disconnected* but not completely *disengaged* from your current earthly body. You are a fortunate observer who has managed to enter an astral journey, not unlike souls who have disconnected during a so-called 'near-death experience.' That experience, incidentally, has nothing to do with near-death and everything to do with astral travel."

I was aware that we were moving—more like rapidly floating—past the edge of what my guide informed me was the second plane. The first plane, or Earth plane, held out-of-body souls who were still attached to what was familiar, or who feared moving on.

The second or *astral* plane—apparently where my vortex was located—was divided into two levels. The lower level included what my Catholic education taught me to refer to as purgatory. The upper level was more of a halfway point between the spirit world and Earth—a place where souls traveled.

As we moved toward the fourth plane, the plane my guide had recently entered, we moved past what many of us had been taught as the idealized view of heaven—the third plane. Those who had entered this plane had been able to recreate their surroundings there to approximate what their earthly religions had taught them was their heaven—instant pleasure and gratification in a perfect Earth with no pain, sorrow, or sickness.

Inquiring why anyone would ever want to move beyond this level, my guide assured me—from experience—that a perfect eternal world was also a perfect eternal bore. To grow further, and move toward the creator, souls must continue to grow, evolve, and purify. I was also assured that, in order to do so, souls must be willing to enter the bodies of many individuals, including those who they know will eventually possess significant evil in their minds.

Apparently sensing my processing of this idea, my guide went on to explain the connection between the soul and the mind. In brief, a soul is pure concentrated cosmic energy. Like other types of energy, it can never be destroyed, but unlike other types of energy, its *form* remains essentially unchanged. As to what that energy does, I was told to think of a body without a soul being like a car without a battery. When human minds sense their conscience, what they are really sensing is the workings of their soul. It is the purview of the soul—or conscience—to attempt to override the evil that rules the hearts and minds of some individuals, and the pure and simple misgivings of others. Obviously, throughout the course of human history, souls have not always been successful in their endeavors, as their efforts have been overridden countless times by truly evil minds. Good and evil, I was assured, exist in the universe as surely as do dark and light, or matter and antimatter. Individuals all serve a purpose, even if that purpose is primarily to act as an education to others.

Sensing my attempts to understand the bigger picture, my guide continued—explaining that since I was disconnected but not disengaged from my human body, a full appreciation of what would be obvious to a disengaged soul would not be possible for me during this astral voyage, but that guidance attempts would continue.

We moved on and again viewed but did not enter the next, or fourth, plane, where it was explained to me that the soul moved on to further exploration beyond earthly confines or the desire for earthly contact.

My guide then further explained that in the fifth plane apparently single souls join other souls as part of a group, but are also able to completely explore the universe, and by the sixth plane they lose form, existing only as intense white light.

"As you now see," I was informed, "we are all ultimately interconnected—at a cosmic level. It is therefore the province of individuals, guided by their souls, to endeavor upon what they believe is relevant assistance in leading other individuals *and their souls* toward ultimately meaningful lives."

As such, to answer what my guide knew was a burning question, I was made aware that the truly important decisions made in the universe are *not* predestined, but they *are* guided. What sense would it make that an all-powerful, all-knowing God would set something in motion just to watch it, being fully aware of the outcome?

I inquired if the universe was infinite and eternal.

"Infinity is a concept you will never understand unless you are a fully disengaged soul," I was told. Attempting to figure it out with a human mind, and then feeling like you are literally bumping up against the inside of your skull, apparently does mean—as I have suspected—that you have reached the very edge of what the human brain can comprehend. This also includes the human notion that everything exists in a single universe. Science, as created by humans, can account for change, but cannot account for creation. This is why science does not really try to prove or disprove the existence of the creator—it can't.

As humans, we are simply not built to fully grasp the concept of *something from nothing*, or understand the singularity of the Big Bang vis-à-vis what came before it, or even what created the substrate. Human science is sometimes right, sometimes wrong, and sometimes doesn't have the faintest clue. Sometimes, though, it needs to be let off the hook for being unable to come up with decent explanations because there *are* none. For example, there is no scientific explanation for déjà vu, because when you sense that something has happened before, it *has*—to your soul. Science, likewise, continues to be frustrated in its attempts to account for the processes of the mind based solely on the materiality of neurobiology—and until it accepts the existence of the soul, the angst will continue. That angst, however, pales in comparison to the amount humans would regularly generate about their own mortality if not for the buffering presence of the soul.

One of the problems of even getting close to understanding the concept of eternity by humans, I was told, was that we perceive time based on an eighty-year lifeline—and mark it with clocks and calendars and defined time blocks like seconds and days and years. Humans started doing this because of sunrises and seasons, but also because it eventually became a way to convene society. Unfortunately, its very convention also simultaneously enslaved us to its defined boundaries. It created a dimension that we could measure, but of which we had no real understanding.

We eventually ended up defining our existence by time, and then we attempted to use reason in an effort to explain it, which means that we ended up backing ourselves into a predefined box that we couldn't and can't reason our way out of. It's why we have trouble wrapping our minds around concepts like *why we aren't regularly visited by spirits.* Souls outside the body don't regularly reveal themselves to us, I was reminded, because eighty years is a mere nanosecond on the timeline of eternity—the timeline that disengaged souls operate on and travel through.

No wonder Schmitty seems to have a better handle on this stuff than I do, I thought. Mind *expansion*—breaking the constraints of time and reason—is really just moving beyond the constraints of mind *contraction,* and my human brain has done plenty of contraction. His has done plenty of the other, so maybe it was open to sensing something when he was in my vortex.

Thinking of Schmitty brought my thoughts back to human existence, and my guide responded to the question that screamed through my consciousness.

"The one you call Joy is a soul that is older than yours. Older souls have substantially more astral experience. This changes the behavior of the individuals they inhabit. Your own human self spends a lot of time analyzing the behavior of individuals, confused about their actions—for example, celebrity worship. Young souls, even while inhabiting humans, are quite intent on establishing connections, and what better way than to attempt to connect with someone who is connected to millions of others—like a celebrity? You also question why Joy left before you turned around to face her on the night you first met. She became aware that you were not yet ready to interact with her."

Where is she now, and why do I have such vivid, incessant dreams of her?

"She is your soul mate, and you are meant to be together."

How did she come to be my soul mate?

"At some point in the astral plane, your souls intertwined."

My consciousness screamed again: *How can I find her?*

"When the time is right, you will come together. Within you is the knowledge necessary to seek her."

I started to ask how to access that knowledge as I became aware of feeling like I was the liquid on the top of a large funnel that was suddenly and rapidly being sucked down into its spout. I tried to grab something—anything—to hold on to where I was. Despair began to set back in again as I realized that my astral journey was ending, and that I was returning to my earthbound self. As I was pulled downward, the intense light I had been enveloped in was rapidly replaced with utter darkness and nothingness . . .

Chapter 17

I awoke slowly—very slowly—coming to the realization that my mouth had tired of the Gobi and had moved on to the Sahara. My bladder was again attempting to kick its way out of my abdomen, and apparently had convinced my brain to attempt the same process with my skull. I sat up, way too quickly, and experienced the same type of headache that some of our post-spinal tap patients feel when they move to a seated position. Decreased cerebrospinal fluid makes just about anyone an unhappy camper. *Christ*, I thought, *why the hell do people drink like this? Why the hell did I drink like this?*

It was time to put a moratorium on the partying, and not just because pickling myself is not part of my lifetime plan. Every bit of the last night's dream—every detail, every nuance—was with me, and I knew I needed to put it into perspective with everything else that had happened in the last couple of days.

Crawling down the ladder from my top bunk, I noted that everyone else was still fast asleep. Opening the door to the garage that adjoined the bunkhouse, I noted that Gus had already been up and had put on a pot of coffee, but was nowhere to be seen—probably out for a walk. After pouring a cup and reveling in the first gulp, I walked around the side of the garage and let my bladder have its way.

Finishing the cup of coffee, I downed my usual antioxidants, then pulled on running shorts, a light T-shirt that I had cut open at the neck, and a pair of New Balance shoes. I laughed at myself as I donned the shirt, thinking about last night's dream. For years I had jokingly told people that the reason I hated anything tight around my neck is that I must have been hanged in a previous life.

I had been running in pretty much the same model of shoes since high school track, and I loved the way they felt and how long a pair would last. Today I was going to let them haul me through the hurt that I knew would last for ten minutes or so, until I burnt off the effects of last night's revelry.

Taking off down the gravel driveway, a nice blast of pine scent did wonders to soothe my aching head. As I pushed forward down to where the driveway crossed the creek, I could really begin to see the devastation that the fire had left. After experiencing any sort of major event, we all learn to progress toward what eventually becomes a new normal, and I knew this would happen here, but the charred remains of the beautiful pine forest that I had known for years still came as quite a shock.

Coming up the logging road, I could see Gus walking toward me.

"Damn shame, isn't it?" he said. I jogged in place beside him.

"Sure is," I noted. "Hopefully they'll find out what happened."

Gus nodded and kept walking back toward camp while

I continued my run down the logging road, literally looking over my shoulder for would-be assailants. My muscles were loosening up as blood laced with caffeine kept moving through, though my head was taking its time in coming around. It was about two and a half miles to the end of the logging road and back to camp, and by the time I got back and sat down, I felt that I had done enough retribution for the previous night's behavior.

Everyone was up by that time except the college boys, and Schmitty was already frying up potatoes and onions, to which he had added about a dozen scrambled eggs. Steve was already halfway through a beer, and Gus was on his third cup of coffee. For me, the endorphins had just begun to kick in. I had never found the actual process of running particularly enjoyable, but the physical benefits and the endorphin rush at the end made the effort well worth it.

Schmitty stirred the frying mass of food and announced: "Doc, we are going into Bemidji when we finish breakfast to pick up some supplies and a few new chairs, and then we'll hit the water so you can get in some fishing time before you have to head out later this afternoon."

"Sounds good," I said. "I'll ride along."

We made quick work of Schmitty's breakfast treat, and Schmitty, Steve, Dan, and I piled into the Blazer for the trip into town.

Bemidji had at least one big-box store where we could pick up the supplies we needed and chairs to replace their fallen comrades. The city itself sits near the east-west center of the state and about a quarter of the way down from the northern border, guarded by Paul Bunyan and Babe the Blue Ox. The trip in took us past a flat expanse of birch trees, small ponds, random grazing cattle, and all manner of pines. As we passed into town, road signs announced the path east to Grand Rapids, west to Crookston, and north to International Falls. Further east and just south of Grand Rapids sat Duluth, and south of us sat Brainerd, with mid-state Saint Cloud and south-state Mankato in a straight line below Brainerd.

The entire state of Minnesota boasts some incredible topography, especially going from north to south. My personal favorite drive is following the Mississippi River from Stillwater just east of the Twin Cities past Hastings, Red Wing, and Wabasha, and down to Winona, which is east of Rochester. The final leg of the trip, from Winona through La Crescent at the state border, boasts magnificent scenery that is hard to match anywhere.

We finished our foraging at the big box and headed for the edge of town. Steve made us stop at a gas station to pick up enough ice to keep his beer cold when we were out on the water. I hit the mobile phone store and grabbed a replacement cell phone—fortunately programmable to my existing number. We headed home to what awaited us . . .

The predator slunk along its path, with little regard for anything other than its prey. Its vacant eyes gave no clue as to where it was moving. Sixty million years of evolution had done very little to modify its appearance—sunken eyes and thick slime and sharp teeth acting as its assets in predation. A sudden flash and rapid flickering movement caught its eye, triggering primitive reflexes. The predator rapidly closed in on its prey, opened its strong jaws, and clamped down.

As it tried to swim away, however, it was pulled forward by a much stronger force—one that had evolved at least slightly more than the predator—and Schmitty was able to land the five-pound northern pike.

"Nice fish, man," Steve yelled from the boat he and I were in, which had just pulled up next to Schmitty's craft.

"He put up a nice fight," observed Schmitty, "and given that we have enough meat in camp, I'm going to send him back to the depths." He unhooked the fish and dropped it back into the lake. We stayed out a couple of hours and managed to hook five more northerns and a walleye. The northerns in this lake always seemed to have a hard time resisting a medium-sized Mepps Syclops lure. We also hooked a decent bass, quickly released because bass season was still two weeks away.

We pulled the boats up on shore, and the other guys walked ahead of Schmitty and me as we made it back to camp. I filled him in on my astral experience from the night before.

"That surprises me, man. I thought you weren't into that shit."

"I'm not—though I did some reading about it recently, so I suppose it was on my mind."

Back at camp, it was about 2 p.m. and time for me to hit the road. I wanted to get home to do some research, especially involving astral travel, that I couldn't handle doing on a smartphone. Besides, I had also agreed to stop by Saint John's and fill in my profs on the progress of my "assignment."

Another meal of fried fish and a protracted "Minnesota good-bye" later, I was back in the Mustang and out on the road. I didn't mind driving the Blazer, but this was much more my idea of fun.

I punched down the accelerator to let the four-barrel carb suck in some gas, and the tach needle in the Rally Pac shot upward. The Rally Pac was an optional clock-tachometer pod that bolted over the steering column behind the steering wheel. It was one of around one hundred options that you could buy from your dealer and add to the car back in 1965. Amazingly, there was an available nine-inch black-and-white TV, among other unusual options, such as a lighted pony ornament for the grill and a reverb unit for the sound system. Being a fanatic of all things Mustang, I had been collecting this crap off of the Internet for years and had recently written a feature on it for a monthly Mustang magazine. I considered the whole thing a hobby. My buddies—more accurately, I suspect—considered it an obsession.

My phone rang. Putting it up to my ear, I heard a voice say, "Have any more blowouts, chief?"

"Luckily, no, Frank," I answered. "To what do I owe the pleasure?"

"Just calling to suggest you keep an eye on your tires, bud. My friend—the one who knows about such things—tells me he's 98 percent certain that your 'road hazard' was actually a knife."

"Thanks—I think," I replied. "I appreciate the call back."

"No problem, man. Keep an eye on those tires and keep it between the ditches."

"Will do," I said as I ended the call. *Just add it to the list of everything else that makes no sense*, I thought. I realized there was nothing I could do about it at that point, anyway. Schmitty and I had decided not to report the cherry-picker shooting incident just yet. We didn't want to be placed in the woods with it near the time of the fire, which was still under investigation, and if my blowout had any ties to any of this . . .

Saint John's University is located in central Minnesota, close to the city of Saint Cloud, on an idyllic 3,200-acre campus named Collegeville. It has a Roman Catholic religious affiliation and was established in 1857—a year before Minnesota officially became a state. Its sister school, the College of Saint Benedict, is located in nearby Saint Joseph. Students can access activities, classes, and the resources of both schools.

The "Harvard of the Pines" indeed was a great place to go to school. No matter how high my ACT score was, or how good my high school grades were, I was never going to be admitted by the "Harvard of the East," and I can honestly say I didn't want to. Being a white Midwestern farm kid with no great family means or ties meant that my record, and a résumé full of extracurriculars, was useless to the Ivy League. As far as I was concerned, the Ivy League was just as useless to me. Saint John's was a haven, with an incredible campus and stellar professors—including my favorite, Alan Tebbins from the history department.

The above considered, during school I always thought it was ironic that some of my professors still felt that such a kid—who *earned* his credentials, and paid his way through college—should feel some sense of "privilege." Either they didn't know my background well enough or they had a totally different concept of privilege than I had. I suspect it was the latter, which, to be fair, would best be discussed in further detail with them. It might have been helpful, though, to have had at least one of them along back in the day when I was driving a rusty Ford Maverick held together with wire, tape, and conviction—especially on the memorable weekend when I blew out three of the four bald tires that supported the thing. Being told that I was somehow privileged, I had suspected back then, was supposed to make me feel guilty about something. I could never figure out exactly what—maybe because I was too busy delaying gratification.

To this day, other than being born in the United States, I don't consider myself privileged—nor do I feel the least bit guilty. I do feel fortunate that I did not grow up hungry—though on the farm we all had jobs to do. I do feel blessed that I have lived an exciting and productive life. Beyond that,

I have worked to pave every inch of my own journey, which means to me that I can honestly harbor no guilt—though I probably do have a few remnants left over from growing up Catholic. (No one can promise that being religious is supposed to be easy.) In spite of the whining that surrounded me when I was growing up, this also means that I do not now, nor will I ever, consider myself a victim of anything or of anyone. *Damn*, I thought, *there I go, all countercultural again.*

I pulled off the freeway and onto the long road leading into Collegeville. I wasn't too far down the road when the imposing façade of the Abbey Church came into view.

As I pulled into campus and into a visitor's parking spot near the music building, I passed one of the dorms. *Ah, Mary Hall*, I thought; *some great memories there. I wonder if they ever changed out those old medicine cabinets.*

As residents of Mary Hall, it hadn't taken us long to figure out how to put a few of its quirks to good use. One involved the old medicine cabinets that were mounted in the walls back-to-back between rooms. You could only get away with this trick once, maybe twice, before the guys in the next room were no longer unwitting.

The trick involved a can of hairspray and a small flame. The old cabinets had a small slot in them, where, in the days of removable-blade razors, the used blades could be deposited. We had discovered that the slots in these cabinets were also back-to-back.

Step one: Open cabinet door. Step two: Have can of hairspray and small flame readily at hand. Step three: Knock loudly enough on back of cabinet until guys next door open their own cabinet door. Step four: Hold flame next to razor blade slot and push down on hairspray can nozzle. Step five: Observe torching flame enter room next door through cabinets. Step six: Run like hell or be prepared to offer peace offering of beer.

Other prospective engineering students had also used their powers of observation to note that the gap between Mary Hall's dorm room doors and the hallway floor was at an exacting tolerance so as to allow further physics experimentation in particle dispersion techniques. The open edge of a medium-sized paper bag filled with shaving cream fit perfectly under said door, and when said bag was stomped on simultaneously by both feet, said shaving cream displayed uniform particle dispersion properties. Step six: Run like hell.

Third-floor rooms were also discovered to have perfect balcony-to-ground distance with which to verify physics calculations involving the equations of constant acceleration, even with large objects that had formerly resembled a couch. Step one: Invite everyone you know over for a party. Step two: Sneak in a keg. Step three: Party all night. Step four: Realize that something someone has been smoking has now reduced your couch to rapidly developing ash. Step five: Get four guys to hoist couch over edge of balcony to test physics equation. Step six: Lie like hell.

As I walked around campus, familiar feelings rushed back in a torrent. The only difficulty I ever had when coming back to Saint John's was the nagging feeling that I just wanted to be a student again—but, at times, who doesn't? Thinking through it, though, always made me realize that the feeling was about the simplicity of that time, more so than attending classes or pulling all-nighters. Life was kind of like sedimentary rock, adding on layers as time went by—not necessarily a bad thing, but sometimes a deterrent to remembering the simplicity underneath.

A better simile on life for me was my own view of life being like a thick book, loaded with chapters telling a story that built on itself. Some chapters would be whimsical and pleasurable, whereas others would veer off in a different direction. As life progressed, the pages of that book would become imprinted in your memory. Like a book, those pages could be opened and reread, or the story could move on in a linear fashion. Sometimes a reread of certain passages could be beneficial to gaining needed perspective—but, like remakes of anything (*Planet of the Apes*, anyone?), some things were best left alone. As to leaving things alone—for example, biological families—one could simply view those chapter pages as being glued together. They couldn't be removed from the book, but they also didn't require a reread. The best lessons learned in life, including what *not* to do when one becomes an adult, will continue to stand out without the reread.

I walked on through the parking lot of the science building—former home of the table chemist—and down to the sunken football field we always referred to as the "natural bowl." I can't imagine a more idyllic place to play or watch a football game, and the Johnnies always put on a great show.

Until my last visit here for a football game, I had a concern that the irreverent, outlaw, wildly attired student group at Saint John's—known as the Rat Pack—may have fallen victim to the ravages of political correctness. The Rats had been around for generations and we Johnnies had rotated through, passing the gauntlet on to the next generation. Seeing them alive and well reaffirmed my faith in Saint John's—an incredible place of learning, where no one was required, or allowed (certainly back then), to have a stick up their ass.

Swinging around the massive Warner Palaestra athletic facility, I made my way up to the bookstore. I always liked to grab a couple loaves of Johnny Bread, made by the resident monks, and to be sure they had enough copies of my book for the shelves.

I left with the bread and walked past Luke Hall, former basement home of Saint John's first campus bar, and made my way to the main quadrangle building and the meeting with my professors.

The quad had been a part of Saint John's since the 1880s. A traditional quadrangle is essentially a central courtyard with an arrangement of buildings on four sides. Early on, this one apparently was the largest educational building west of the Mississippi River. It had served multiple purposes over the years, including housing students, seminarians, administrators, and several classrooms. It had also housed our refectory dining area, and it was impossible to walk into the place without thinking about the crazy amount of food we used to eat as college students.

After going into the main entrance, I took a left down a long hallway until I came to a small door that I suspect most people walked right past without noticing. In fact, as a student, I don't really remember ever having noticed it myself, as it blended right into the woodwork.

I slowly descended a circular stone staircase one level down to a landing where another small door faced me. After knocking, I opened the door, and there, in the middle of a small room seated around a round wooden table, were four people who had influenced me immensely at a very formative time in my life.

"Derek, Derek—come on in!" Alan Tebbins fairly shouted.

I looked around and noted a shaft of light coming in from a small window at ceiling level that was opened to the outside. Cigar smoke from the table—littered with playing cards—was wafting in a ghostlike stream up and out the window. A small table on casters sat in the corner of the room, and on top of it were a number of bottles containing bourbon, brandy, whiskey, and vodka.

"Would you like a drink?" asked Alan.

"Actually, just a diet cola if you have one," I said.

"That we do, as Jane, for reasons I've never been able to understand, likes to mix her vodka with *diet* cola," said Alan as he handed me the can.

Jane Grundy laughed. "In my lifelong search for the truth, I've never been able to understand it either," the philosopher quipped. "Some things just *are*."

"I remember, as a kid, when Tab was introduced as one of the first diet colas," offered Robert Liebfried, my analytical but excitable and high-energy economics professor. "Great marketing campaign—for people who wanted to keep *tabs* on their weight." He stole a glance at Pat Calloway. "Sold like crazy until the FDA got involved."

Pat Calloway, despite being built like a linebacker, was an incredibly laid-back kind of guy for a political scientist. "We'll save the larger ongoing discussion of the role of government regulation for another day. Suffice it to say, regarding Tab, as I remember, the FDA got their act straight and eventually revoked the mandatory warning labels."

"Twenty years later," Liebfried muttered under his breath.

I laughed out loud. "Can I quit my job and come back here tomorrow and re-enroll? Medicine is interesting and challenging, but it's never intellectually stimulating to me in this sort of way."

Alan looked at me. "All of us here knew that you certainly weren't a typical student—which is why we answered your query the way we did and invited you here to discuss it. We talked about it for quite some time after we received it and realized that we share some of your same frustrations. I know you pretty well from your time here at Saint John's, Derek, and also from the time we have spent together since you graduated. I suspect that our views may differ somewhat as to solutions for the issues you raise, but I also suspect that our goals are quite similar, actually. Feel free to ask us any questions you would like. We will offer our views, and since we aren't representing the university here, we can be as open as we want. Primarily, Derek, we would like to hear what *you* have to say."

I was glad to hear him start out the discussion that way. I have always felt, in the end, that people of good character—no matter what their political persuasion—have the best overall intentions in mind for everyone. Just thinking about that brought an immense feeling of calmness to my psyche—like a light warm breeze blowing across my face. It became apparent to me, just then, that I would forever be affected—in a uniquely positive way—by my astral experience from the night before. Allowing myself to believe that we are all ultimately interconnected gave me a tremendous sense of relief—a sense that we might actually be able to move beyond the polarity we had managed to create. I realized then that what we needed to talk about was just that—how we move beyond the polarity. I posed the question.

"You need compromise to avoid polarity, and in order to compromise, you need dialogue," offered Pat Calloway. "Right now, we don't have any real dialogue," he said. "Political party designations have evolved into the ultimate straw man setup, where as soon as someone gets identified as a member of a particular political persuasion, they are branded as a member of the opposition and the shouting begins. Everyone starts to throw around their own set of facts—the ones that support the narrative that they have been spoon-fed. This happens on both sides of the fence. It's like some sort of political Tower of Babel where no one understands anyone else—not because they are speaking different languages, but because they are simply not trying to hear each other.

"And," he continued, "the Twitter-feed culture and sound-bite world we live in does nothing to help mitigate the problem. I see it all the time with my students and it drives me bananas. How the hell can anyone form a decent *informed* opinion when none of the daily news they receive exceeds 140 characters?"

"I'll agree with that," Alan offered. "When it comes to students, I'm constantly fighting the 'old fart' battle with myself, wondering what things to stand firm on, and what things to just let go. I think I have finally decided that it's a waste of time to try to force them to identify locations on a United States map, when most of them are used to just pulling out their smartphones and looking them up.

"I don't think I'll ever get the Twitter thing, however," he continued. "I have always been as much of a social justice guy as most of my current students appear to be, but the things they seem to accept without a fight—like Twitter-feed news or revisionist history—really worry me. I'm thinking about offering a course on revisionist history, if only to solidify the point that driving true bigotry and racism underground isn't going to cure it. We need completely accurate historical accounts to remind us where we have succeeded, as well as where we have failed. 'Cleaning it up' does nothing to further the cause."

"I couldn't agree more," I said, "especially when something like the topic of privilege is thrown into a conversation. It is a topic that I *will* discuss if we start out with its true historical perspective and move forward to where we are now—but I *won't* if it's being thrown out by someone to prove how enlightened they are, or being used as a PC way to suppress my opinion. If the latter does happen, I simply ask that individual to tell me what they know about how I got to where I am. The conversation usually ends right there, which is good, because it is important for me to avoid responding viscerally, just as it is for someone else to avoid tossing out potentially polarizing sound bites in the first place. I personally can't propose the expression of all answers, but I can propose the expression of all opinions."

"Back to Alan's point, it's amazing, really," mused Robert. "We have this culture of people who feel that they are so connected, when in fact they are terribly disconnected."

"I think that is an incredibly important point," I observed. "One of my concerns, in life as well as in the practice of medicine, is that we have lulled individuals into a very concerning sense of complacency—where they literally begin to expect that everything will get fed to them. Where they also begin to feel that no matter how badly they behave, someone—their doctor or their government—will eventually bail them out. Personally, I'm not against doctors or government. I'm against too much of either one."

"Society *should* be responsible for its failings," Alan stated a bit sharply, "and government is the vehicle by which it is held accountable. If society is failing to educate its children properly, or allowing certain individuals to prosper exorbitantly as others fail, then it—through its government—holds the moral responsibility to police itself."

"Here's my take," Jane Grundy offered, "and *of course* it's based on philosophy. I read your book, Derek, and was pleased to see that you ended it with a quote from Rousseau. Obviously you believe in the concept of the social contract. As you well know, the concept essentially originated with Plato and Socrates, and was largely expounded on by Hobbes, Locke, and of course Rousseau. It is very difficult for anyone to argue against the idea that, in order to form a society, individuals must consent to submit to the rule of that society—even potentially surrendering some of their freedoms—as a contract to protect their remaining individual rights. Of course, some modernists have attempted to twist it to fit their own narrative, but that's no big surprise.

"The gist of the concept, as it applies here," she continued, "is what *legitimate* authority should a state hold over an individual? As societies become more complex, this becomes a very slippery-slope issue. Personally, I am concerned that individuals now seem to be more willing to surrender more of their freedoms to the state, not to help protect their other individual rights, but in exchange for the state to somehow *guarantee* them. While I agree with Alan in general that societies should be responsible for certain inequities, I'm beginning to feel that we need to become much more specific in our thinking as to what societies should truly be responsible for. Both sides of the political fence obviously champion the idea of personal freedom. The divergence point is on who is responsible to pay when there are costs involved—the individual, or the collective?"

"I'm going to quote Patrick Henry here, and only to preface making a point," remarked Robert, saying: "The Constitution is not an instrument for the government to restrain the people—it is an instrument for the people to restrain the government—lest it come to dominate our lives—"

"I'm sorry to interrupt here, Robert," I said, "but before you go on, based on that quote, I want to pose a question that I hope the rest of your remarks may help answer."

"Go ahead," he nodded.

"Thank you. I occasionally get a vision of some sort of behavioral Laffer curve, based on excess government intervention in society, where at various tipping points people simply give up and acquiesce. Does anyone here ever worry that when *every* car in America has a required backup camera tied to automatic brakes, that people will eventually stop turning around at all to look when they put their vehicles in reverse?"

"So that means we shouldn't equip cars with them?" asked Alan.

"I don't know yet," I said. "I do know that there will

be a lot of wrangling trying to figure out who or what to blame when someone gets run over—is it the driver, or the pedestrian, or is it the camera not being good enough? We seem to be evolving into some sort of *individualistic* society where we want to be free to do anything we want, and then blame society and have it pick up the tab when the shit hits the fan. For some things, society may be at fault. Sometimes, when bad things happen, it is simply individuals who are at fault—not society, or lack of education, or any other commonly exercised excuse—and those individuals should be held responsible.

"Better yet," I continued, "they should hold themselves responsible. A large segment of our population unfortunately seems to be convinced that bad behavior can usually be justified by circumstance, and that circumstance can usually be justified by some failing of society rather than the failing of an individual. As I look at it, this country was built by responsible individuals, and individual responsibility remains necessary to maintain its viability. It is absolutely necessary for our society to maintain a safety net, but to keep the net from getting overloaded we need to continue to stress that individuals are ultimately responsible for fixing their problems—not government."

Robert cleared his throat. "The point I'm trying to make here is an economic one," he said. "I, too, believe in societal responsibility, but as an economist I'm also a realist when it comes to knowing that if your well is going to quench your thirst, it has to have some water in it. Economically speaking, the greatest historical hedge against poverty has been free market capitalism. We can debate, and we *have* debated, the pros and cons of this system ad nauseam—and yes, there are some things we need to fix in it, including the corporate tax rate and the enforcement thereof."

"I'm glad you brought that up," commented Alan. "We could do so much more if we didn't constantly let big corporations off the hook."

"On the corporate enforcement side, I agree," I said. "By extension, given that our society should operate with shared responsibility, perhaps for everyone to understand how the system works, *everyone* who is in it should pay some rate of federal tax—however small or however large. As demand for services increases, then everyone could observe what happens to their taxes. If this occurred, perhaps we could debate cranking up job creation in our economy by bringing our overall corporate tax rate more in line with that of the rest of the industrialized world.

"I don't think the fundamental question anymore is *what* we want," I continued, "but *who* or *what* is best to accomplish it. Going back to the complacency issue, I sometimes think about big government being like a lifeguard at the beach. The safest scenario for children in the water really is a shared responsibility between their parents and the lifeguard. If the lifeguard convinces the parents that she can do the job herself, and they abdicate their responsibility to her and stop watching their children, we all know what the outcome might be. We need to learn to recognize when further intervention actually compounds problems instead of alleviating them. For some reason, however, this society in large part doesn't seem to fear large federal bureaucracy as much as it should—again, I suspect because we've become way too complacent in general. There is a limit to the effective size of anything, and federal government is no exception. We have designated state and local entities for a reason."

"Economically, maintaining those divisions makes sense," added Robert.

"Yes, and it concerns me tremendously," I said, "that big-picture thinking like that seems to have become a victim of political expediency, and at a tremendous cost. Societies need the appropriate amount of both long-term and short-term thinking as well as action to survive and to thrive. For example, trying to adjust our Medicare system to keep it solvent is not akin to 'throwing Grandma off the cliff,' just as finding new sources of revenue to keep it solvent until we can correct it is not akin to 'rampant taxing and spending.' Inherent in this, and in many other issues we struggle with, seems to be the apparent inability of government—as it now stands at the national level—to be able to respond in any meaningful way to the bigger long-term picture. As the apparent arbiter of social justice, it scrambles to respond to all things short term—like building more parks while Rome burns from the inside out."

Pat Calloway slowly stood up. "Our form of government is revered across the world as the model to which most others aspire."

"They may aspire to it," I shot back, "but they would be less enamored in viewing it at the ground level, where they would see that as it now operates, *it just isn't working.* We can try to blame the ineffectiveness of any decent policymaking on the stubbornness of either political party, or we can face the truth. Our federal bureaucracy is so bloated right now that it can't bend over and tie its own shoes. I don't care how fast your racehorse is if you feed her six bales of hay right before the race begins. She is just going to take a big shit and lay down in the stall. Without any real debate on anything, we have no dialogue, and all we end up with is a big stall full of shit—one big polarized stall full of shit."

"Gentlemen," interjected Jane Grundy. "I'm going to sit out this next hand and go outside and catch a breath of fresh air."

She looked at me and tipped her head in a motion toward the door, as she began to walk toward it.

"I'll join you," I said as I followed her up the stairs.

Chapter 18

We walked down the hall and out into the courtyard of the quad. A moderate but welcome cooling breeze was wafting through the pines.

"Getting *warm* enough for you in there?" Jane asked.

"It is heating up," I said, "and in a good way. Did you notice with all the various points we in that room were making, that no one ever once mentioned a tie with any of them to a particular political persuasion? *That* is a debate."

"Do you mind if I ask you a question, Derek?" asked Jane.

"Go right ahead."

"It's been a couple of years since I talked to you, but I sense something different in you—something *deeply* different. I can't exactly put my finger on it, but some time ago I became aware that I possess some sort of extra perception when it comes to reading people. Have you recently had a life-altering experience?"

I started to say no, but something told me to tell her the truth, and I told her all of it—except for anything related to the apparent murder attempts—starting with my first experience in the vortex.

"Incredible—incredible," she remarked. She made me promise to tell her how everything eventually played out.

"I'm really glad that the change I was reading in you is

because of your recent experiences. I was worried that maybe you were in some kind of trouble," she said.

I looked at her quizzically. "Any reason for that?"

"Well . . . I'm dating Dr. Phillips from the chemistry department. He told me something kind of strange yesterday. He said that a guy—somewhat disheveled—wandered into the science building early in the day. He kept walking up and down the halls mumbling, and then occasionally sticking his head into classroom doors. They eventually called security and had him escorted out. Dr. Phillips sent to my phone a picture he had quickly taken as the man was being escorted out, so that if I saw him, I could steer clear and call the police."

"And this applies to me . . . how?"

"As they were dragging him out the door, he kept yelling something that sounded like: 'Derek Mann, Derek Mann—you son of a bitch! I'm going to make you pay!'"

"Another esteemed member of my fan club, I gather?"

"Don't make fun of this, Derek," she pleaded. "Do you know of anyone that is out to harm you?"

"Seriously, not that I'm aware of," I answered. "Could you do me a favor, though?" I asked.

"What's that?" she asked.

"Could you forward that picture to my phone also, for obvious reasons?"

She agreed, I gave her my number, and she texted me the picture.

I received it immediately and took a quick peek at it.

It was a low-quality profile picture of a man whose face had a distant familiarity to it. He was between two guards, and one of his arms was held in a sling. Quite suddenly, I stiffened, as my mind flooded itself with details of a recent dream about a camouflaged figure holding an assault rifle.

"Do you recognize him?" inquired Jane.

"Never seen him before," I lied.

"I'm surprised the police haven't tried to contact you, since it sounded like your name he was yelling."

"Well, I've been running around the state so much the last few days that I wouldn't be surprised if they did try, and the call just didn't go through."

"You *need* to be careful," she said in the most motherly of voices.

"I will," I promised, beginning to suspect that being careful alone was not going to be anywhere close to being enough.

We walked back into the quad and back down the stairs to the little room where my three other professors remained. As we entered, they were all facing away from us—toward the drink table—and appeared to be mixing up libations. As I began to wonder if our conversation was over, or how it might restart, all three of them turned around—smiling—and started clapping.

Sensing the confusion on my face, Alan stepped forward and spoke for them all. "Derek," he said, "we are all so pleased that the practice of medicine has not rotted your brain, and that you have remained a critical thinker. We are all intelligent enough to know that, in this room, the positions on the issues we discussed are likely quite divergent. I suspect that you were aware, as were we, that the words *right* and *left*, or *conservative* and *liberal* were never uttered. What *was* uttered, at the beginning and the end of the conversation that we've had so far, was the *truth*—which is that there will be no end to the polarization we are saddled with unless those who represent us begin acting like *human* beings, and not *political* beings. We can—and likely will—argue about how that can best be accomplished, but at least we will do so in a way where we respect and honor each other's opinions. We can only hope that everyone who represents us in government will choose to do the same."

I looked at each of them and realized again how incredibly fortunate I was to have had them guide me through my college education. "Thank you!" I said sincerely. "Thank you very much! I'll have that drink now—vodka and Tab please."

Jane laughed and mixed me the drink. They each had a couple more as we laughed and talked about the old times, and current times. I stayed with plain Tab after my drink, as I had to drive home—plus, I had something else to do on campus before I left. We eventually said our good-byes, promising to get together soon and go at this again in further depth. As I bade them good-bye to head toward the Alcuin Library, Jane touched my shoulder.

"Derek," she said, "you must promise me something."

"Yes, I will be careful."

"Well—that too," she said, "but there is one more thing. As soon as you get home, you must further investigate Balzac. As you probably know, he is most renowned as a nineteenth century novelist and playwright, so we didn't cover him much in the philosophy realm—though as you may also know, his genre often contributes immensely to the body of philosophy. I don't know why I'm telling you this, but something tells me that you need to do this."

I thanked her, mentally filed the information, and headed across campus. Before heading to the library, I thought I would make a stop at the science building to see if Dr. Phillips was in so I could pick his brain about what Jane said that he saw. I took a right and headed down the hallway toward his office.

Unfortunately, the eraser board on his office door had a note written on it stating that he was going to be off campus for the next two days. As I started to walk back out, I passed by the door to the biology offices and the bulletin board on the wall next to it. A note in the middle of it from Dr. Grundoffer—addressed to his senior students—caught my eye:

> As some of you may know, Saint John's has established a Chair of Critical Thinking. Critical thinking, of course, applies across all disciplines, and requires an objective analysis in the process of forming a judgment. Our primary goal in higher education has always been the development and encouragement of

critical thinking skills, and the objective analyses that are their foundation.

As you move on into the next phase of your life, or your education, I strongly urge you to not only continue to think critically, but also to rebel against the use of anything less than critical thinking by others as they attempt to influence the behavior of society.

As such, I must relate to you a recent experience of mine where, at a large public event, I came across a display regarding climate change. As you students of science are aware, the debate regarding climate change continues—as it should. While we have not yet accurately determined what man's role is in climate change, or what the real risks of climate change may be, there is no doubt that we need to be stalwart stewards in the protection of our Earth—and from there the debate should continue.

It must, however, continue as a debate—and not as a chess piece of political correctness.

At the public event I attended, the climate change exhibit I came across attempted to ascribe a number of recent deleterious occurrences to a very small recent rise in temperature. Of particular note, the exhibit cited on one panel that deer ticks are more active as temperature rises. Next to this was a panel with the bold word *CONSEQUENCE* on the top which outlined the threefold rise in Lyme's disease cases in the *ten*-year period of 2000 to 2010—and that was it—nothing more, other than an obvious correlation-implies-causation sound bite tossed at a sound–bite-consuming public.

My instant furor was twofold. First, what the exhibit noted obviously didn't even approach "junk science"—as presented, it was merely junk. While it is entirely possible that the exhibitor's conclusion could somehow be true, that was far from having been determined. Second, and just as important, have we passed the point where there apparently is no shame associated with this blatant attempt at manipulation?

I eventually managed to locate the originator of the exhibit and left him a response regarding my critique of it. I told him that my own research has indicated that younger individuals are also more active as temperature rises, and therefore I have concluded that this is the reason why hip-hop influences started to flood mainstream pop music during the same time period.

I am still awaiting his response.

The Alcuin Library at Saint John's was built, along with the Engel Science Center, in 1966—long before I arrived on the scene. World-renowned architect Marcel Breuer designed both buildings, as well as the Abbey Church, which was built a few years prior. All three buildings are architectural treasures, with the library holding a nationally recognized book collection. I wasn't going there for the books.

I entered the library and told a staff member what I was looking for. "Sure, we still have those in paper form," I was told.

She found the years I was looking for and reminded me that I could not remove them from the premises, but I was welcome to look through them.

Paging through my old student directories while sitting in the Alcuin was yet another synapse twister. I started in year one and worked my way through. I couldn't help smiling at the faces I recognized—some belonging to people with whom I still held acquaintance, or at least ran into at the yearly reunion events during homecoming.

I stopped smiling when, halfway through year three, I recognized the face, and all of the memories came rushing back to me . . .

Premed courses were—and remain—quite a rigorous subset of undergrad education. They are a set block of courses in the sciences that everyone who applies to medical school needs to complete, obviously the more successfully the better when it comes to application time. Other students majoring in biology, chemistry, physics, or math who aren't on the premed track may be taking the same courses, and they have their own needs for success when it comes to pre-vet, pre-engineering, etc. Needless to say, there is a lot of competition to do well—especially if the class is being graded on a curve.

In junior year, I was in an organic chemistry class that was a required element for anyone on the premed track. As usual, the competition was stiff among the twenty-eight students enrolled in this particular section, and "table chemistry" wasn't going to cut it in this class. I always did well in chemistry, though for some reason I never considered it a strong suit for me. Given that I knew I needed to do well in this class to support my med school application, I remember being on my toes the entire semester—and therefore I'm sure it looked to the others in the class that I was a gunner.

One of the others in the class was a young man named Asmail. I didn't know what his undergrad track was, but it appeared to me, and to most everyone else in the class, that he was struggling. As I recall, about halfway through the semester, he stopped showing up. By the time the semester was over, the scuttlebutt had filtered down to the rest of us in class that he had not simply quit—he was thrown out of the class. None of us would find out until much later that he had been accused of cheating, and apparently it was another class member that had turned him in and had also supplied proof of the infraction. All of it was kept quite confidential, though we later heard that Asmail was convinced that everyone in class knew what had happened right away, and that we were laughing at his expense.

I really didn't know much about Asmail, though when he was in the class I had tried a few times to say hello and strike up a conversation. He really didn't seem interested and kept primarily to himself. Most of the rest of us, despite the competition in the class, joked around a lot about how we were being bent over, and the humor was a welcome relief from the tension.

Shortly after he "quit" the class, I remember running into Asmail a few times as we walked in opposite directions on the sidewalk between the Science Center and Mary Hall. I didn't know that he was on the premed track, and I certainly didn't know why he was no longer in the class. For all I knew, he had decided that he didn't like the class, or didn't need the class, or had just changed directions with his major.

The first time, I had walked up to him, laughed, and said: "Man, am I jealous of you—off that damn hamster wheel known as organic chem!" He had looked at me then with a blank stare that I can still recall. The stare was blank, but what was behind his eyes wasn't. After a few seconds, and without a word, he kept walking.

In my typical way, I felt bad—wondering what *I* had done or said wrong. Of course, rather than just let it go, I vowed that the next time I saw him, I would rectify whatever was wrong—even though I didn't know what was wrong, or if *anything* was wrong.

About a week later we crossed paths again and "Mr. Humor" took another shot at it. "Man, we are getting killed in that class—you dropped at the right time."

This time he just kept walking, and I heard him yell a word three times successively that about a month later my brain finally identified as *schadenfreude.* By that time, Asmail had dropped all of his classes and had disappeared from Saint John's with no forwarding address. I had no way to ask him why he felt that I was somehow gaining pleasure from his misfortune.

That was the end of that—or so I thought until now. It apparently had taken a while, but for some reason the man must have eventually just snapped. *It made no sense as to why it had taken this long,* I thought. *Something must have set him off . . . but what?* What would have pushed him over the edge to try to exact revenge on me this many years later? What would be different now?

My book . . . ? It had been picked up by a large national book retailer, so he may have run across a copy of it, or read something about it online. I knew I had pissed off a few people before with things I had written, but seriously . . .

It suddenly occurred to me that it wasn't about what I had written, but what I had *become.* Once he had gotten bounced out of the organic chemistry class for cheating, his med school aspirations were over, and in his mind, I was to blame. A sad circumstance of cultural separation, yes, but the man obviously harbored deeper demons.

I didn't remember much of my college calculus, but I didn't need anything that complex in order to put two and two together to arrive at a conclusion regarding what I suspected was Asmail's current behavior.

Chapter 19

Leaving Saint John's, I drove quickly until I got closer to home. Deep in thought, I passed by the Scott County Fairgrounds, a favorite hangout of my youth. Suppressing the desire to detour through them, I motored on. By now I'd had about enough "vacationing" and was ready to experience some solitude, or so I thought. I rolled the Stang up the driveway and put the horse in its stall. Opening up the trunk, I retrieved my backpack from its home of the last couple of days. Walking into the house, my first goal was to brew a big pot of hot java.

Right now, I needed a cup of coffee like Mom used to make. With her version of Mississippi Mud, you never stirred with a spoon because you were afraid all you'd pull back out was the handle. I put the backpack down front forward on the table next to my laptop and headed to the kitchen.

I put the mud on to brew and fired up the laptop. It was time to try to make some sense out of the bits and pieces of information gained from the vortex that were pounding around in my brain.

It was also time to finally pull on the big-boy pants and come to grips with my dreams and my feelings about Joy, and what I planned to do about them.

I drained eight ounces of mud into a heavy cup, avoided the spoon, and sat down at the laptop desk. My cell phone began its familiar warble, and when I was about to silence it, I noticed that it was Schmitty on the other side. "How's your head, man?" he chirped smugly.

"Just peachy," I uttered.

"I know you're probably home, and that you've got shit to do, but listen to Schmitty for a minute. Fire investigators are leaning toward our blaze up here as being deliberately set. They've closed off the remaining woods, but they apparently haven't run across anything else yet, so that bastard is probably still out there somewhere. Be effing careful."

"You know me, man. 'Careful' is my middle name."

"That's why I'm worried, buddy."

I hung up the phone and felt instantly guilty about the omission of the truth that I had just perpetrated. I would tell Schmitty soon enough what I found out at Saint John's, and everything else I knew, but first I wanted to sort through it all by myself. After the session with my professors, my brain felt amazingly clear—more so than in years. Perhaps now it would be truly open to a further understanding of what I thought I had seen in the vortex, and during my astral travel—and perhaps now I might actually be able to interpret it. Truth was, I wanted to open up my mind to everything I'd seen to be able to begin my search for Joy.

I closed my eyes and tried to recall everything I could about my experiences. If they assisted in any way in helping me find Joy, then I was ready to put any of my remaining skepticism aside.

The astral guide had told me that the vortex was the

repository of my soul—and that very few individuals had ever stumbled into their vortex as a united human body and soul while *conscious* of being in it, or had stayed there long enough to experience it. Quite an intriguing thought as to who the others had been. People who deduced what the vortex was? People who didn't? People who used it for the purposes of good? People who didn't?

I had to assume that the vortex effect was the same on those individuals as it was on me. My guide had informed me that the innate abilities I possessed and thought about when I was in the vortex would be amplified—at least temporarily. This had certainly *seemed* to be the case with my guitar playing and diagnostic experience. Could it have been the same with, say, a da Vinci? Could the man who loved to travel from Florence to nearby Pisa and spend time in its leaning tower have found a spot where the fifteenth century equivalent of "Spill the Wine" was playing? Might give us an explanation for those medieval helicopter drawings. Or perhaps for an incredible mathematical sequence seen throughout nature and "discovered" by an earlier denizen of that city—Leonardo of Pisa, otherwise known as Fibonacci.

None of this, however, gave me an explanation of what I needed for *me.*

What about the second time I went up into the vortex—the time I specifically thought about nothing but Joy and how to find her? Did something get amplified that time?

Before the shots were fired and I was pulled back out of the vortex, I had begun to see some familiar outlines of a city street and of a woman. Were my *thinking* abilities being amplified, or maybe some *psychic* ability?

I assured myself that it was not any sort of psychic ability, because far from that, I don't even get subtle. I do, however, possess a fairly decent ability to reason, so perhaps the amplification of that ability is what led me to be able to see what I saw. If indeed that was the case, I thought, then as long as that amplification wasn't temporary, I should be able to again pull up a vision of the street view I had witnessed.

Buoyed by that thought, I opened my eyes, took a deep breath, and closed them again. I let my mind wander back to the cherry picker and the second trip up into the vortex. I even tipped my head back as I tried to take myself back to the vision I had seen.

Again and again, I tried to focus on a vision that simply would not come into focus. The more I tried, the more frustrated I became. Eventually it just made my head hurt.

I opened my eyes and went into the kitchen, opened the refrigerator, and grabbed a can of orange juice. Chugging it, I walked back to the laptop desk. I looked down at the Saint John's University calendar that the laptop was sitting on.

Balzac . . ., I thought. I'll clear my head and keep my promise to Jane at the same time.

What the hell would we do without Google? I mused as I punched in *Balzac.* I wasn't sure what I was supposed to gain from this exercise, but Jane didn't seem to know either. I knew a little bit about Balzac but not a lot, and as I read on, I smiled about some interesting personality similarities between the two of us, so maybe this was where Jane was going.

In European literature of the nineteenth century, Frenchman Honore de Balzac was considered to be one of the founders of realism, largely because of his unfiltered view of society. Apparently his penchant for independent thinking also made his path through life a bit less than smooth. His signature work, *La Comedie Humaine,* was also said to have mirrored some of his own difficulties in life.

As I was perusing the background for his work, I found it all quite interesting until I came across *Louis Lambert*, and then it went from interesting to intriguing. The setting for most of this fictional story was a school at Vendome, France—which happened to be the same school attended by Balzac when he was a boy. The story concentrated largely on the metaphysical ideas of the story's protagonist—ideas which have apparently led many to believe that Balzac himself may have had some *astral experience*.

All of this had to be more than circumstantial! I quickly pressed forward, searching for some possible connection—anything that would lead me in the right direction.

After about an hour, my head hurt again and I went to the refrigerator for another orange juice. I sat down again at the laptop, and for whatever reason punched in Vendome, and pulled up an image of the school that Balzac attended.

I don't know how or why it hit me suddenly, but something about the architecture I was looking at apparently got a complex series of neuronal interconnections to play on the same team long enough to feed me a visual—a visual of a warehouse district. This was one that I realized was quite close by, and where I suddenly was certain that I'd seen a beautiful woman walking when I was in the vortex. I pulled up some images on Google Street View, and they matched my visual perfectly.

I must've sensed something at the time that made me decide to leave a note as to my intentions, and, with no paper or pen in sight, I left a block message on the open computer screen: GOING TO SEARCH FOR JOY.

That message, and the street views I had been observing, were also big enough to be picked up by the broadcast camera in the front of my backpack . . .

Chapter 20

The Warehouse District in Minneapolis is a common name for a neighborhood in the North Loop of the central part of the city. Part of it is listed on the National Register of Historic Places. The North Loop itself is close to the Minneapolis central business district and sits between the Mississippi River and downtown Minneapolis. In the northeast part of the neighborhood sits James Rice Park, which lies close to the river and attracts walkers, joggers, bikers, and anyone who enjoys beautiful views. Further south, between the Plymouth and Broadway Avenue bridges, is a biking and walking trail that runs right alongside the river. Over the years, as the district has developed, it has attracted quite a number of businesses, as well as stellar dining and shopping.

I motored the Stang down Highway 169 and then headed east on 394 toward downtown Minneapolis and the Warehouse District. Target Field, home of the Minnesota Twins, loomed large on my left as I came up on Washington Avenue and then proceeded forward on Third Avenue North. A few blocks to the southeast sat the First Avenue nightclub, Prince's main stage in the eighties.

After I had left home, I had simply driven to my destination, with no idea of what I was going to do when I arrived there. As I arrived in downtown Minneapolis, the ridiculous nature of my quest suddenly struck me. What was I going to do, drive around until I found her?

Third Avenue North ended at First Street North, so I took a left and started driving through the Warehouse District. It was lunchtime, and diners and shoppers were wandering the sidewalks. Looking ahead, a red brick multistory tower rose at the dead end of the street. I recognized it as part of the Star Tribune printing building. I'd seen it before, but I could sense that the recesses of my brain were trying to make a connection to something deeper—perhaps to some other piece of architecture I had recently viewed.

As I came upon it and the street ended, I took a left on North Eighth Avenue and then another left on North Second Street, essentially going around the block.

I have no idea how many times I drove that same loop, scanning the streets until my eyes got tired.

Eventually I gave up, turned back onto Third Avenue North, and took a right on Washington Avenue. On my left I passed Bunkers, a Minneapolis live-music institution.

Coming to a stop at Washington and Plymouth, I took a right on Plymouth, and then a right on West River Parkway. Just as I turned onto the parkway, I noticed a small park that overlooked the river, so I took a quick left and pulled in. Parking was fortunately ample, only because it was the middle of a weekday. I had no idea what made me stop there; maybe my brain just needed a rest.

Sitting in the car with my eyes closed for a few minutes did the trick, and, refreshed, I got out of the car and walked down the path that led to a paved trail along the river. A fresh breeze was whistling through the tops of the tall basswoods that populated the park. The Plymouth Avenue Bridge loomed almost overhead as I made my way down to the trail, which, at this point, ran right up to the edge of the river bank. The mighty Mississippi was tumbling over itself, as it particularly does during spring in Minnesota, moving around 1.6 million gallons of water per second. *How in hell did I remember that statistic*, I thought, *when I have no idea what I ate for breakfast yesterday morning?*

Deep in thought, I almost missed the movement that I had sensed in the vegetation—which I noted out of the corner of my left eye. Instinctively, I quickly stopped and backed up two steps. I was at the edge of a line of thick young trees, which sat just above the paved trail near the river. The trees ended at the edge of the path I was walking on.

After waiting a few seconds that seemed like an eternity, I peered out through the edge of the tree line. My first sensation was that my heart had stopped beating completely—quickly followed by an uncontrolled gallop. On the cement path, walking away from me and just about to walk under the bridge, was a tall brunette whose shape instantly lit up my memory banks. Was it *her*, or was my mind playing tricks on me? Even though my dreams about her were extremely vivid, it had been a few years since I'd actually seen her.

She was walking slowly and wearing headphones, the heavy noise-canceling type that usually have a built-in radio. Between her and me, emerging from the tree line, was another figure whose face I could see just well enough to note its similarity to the picture of Asmail I had just seen at Saint John's. He quickly peered back and forth as if to see if anyone else was in the vicinity, while I literally shook my head trying to figure out what he was doing there.

Seemingly satisfied, he crept down the short distance of grassy bank and onto the paved path, closing the distance between himself and the woman. As he did so, he reached into his jacket and pulled out—to my horror—what I realized with absolute certainty was a handgun with a silencer.

My certainty about the identity of both individuals was not as absolute as that of the gun, but with what apparently was about to happen, it didn't matter.

The human brain is a truly amazing instrument. Given choices, it can take days or weeks or years to formulate an action plan. Given a split second, it can also do the same. The one second I gave mine formulated a rapid realization. The only chance I had to save this woman was to quickly and quietly move to close the gap between her and her would-be assailant, and when close enough, to strike as quickly as possible to subdue him before he turned and shot me first.

As I quietly snuck along the grass line between the trees and the path, I simultaneously blocked the building rage within that I *knew* this coward, and that he apparently had decided to best extract his revenge on me by first killing what he knew was most dear to me. But how did he find her?

As I moved closer, I realized that the coward could pull the trigger at any time, or wait until he was right behind his target, on whom he was closing quickly. I also knew that, as I got closer, at any second he could sense my presence and turn and pull the trigger. My only hope was staying on the grass and getting close enough to where I could take off at a sprint and tackle him before he could get off a shot at either one of us.

At less than ten yards away, I made my move. I got to the edge of the path and pushed off hard with my right foot, like coming out of the blocks in my track days. Knowing I wasn't quite as fast now as I was then was less than comforting, but at least I was still wearing the same shoes.

If you have ever been in a car accident, you will understand what the next couple of seconds were like, as I—in a mental slow-motion haze—motored toward the bastard on the path.

When I had closed a bit more than half of the distance between us, it was obvious that he heard me coming. His body began swinging to the left—toward me—as his right arm with gun in hand swung a larger arc around his body.

Six feet away from him, I pushed off hard with my right foot and took a flying leap.

As I dove into him, I jammed my right shoulder in under the ribs on his left side. I heard a groan and a muffled gunshot next to my ear, simultaneously feeling a sharp stabbing pain shoot through the middle of my chest.

We rolled across a few feet of gravel, and after that it was falling and rolling down toward the river on a bank of large, heavy rock—and an incredibly hard impact followed by sudden and absolute blackness . . .

Chapter 21

After enough time—who knows how long—I began to come to grips with the idea that being dead wasn't altogether a bad thing. My experience with the astral guide had removed any fear of afterlife unknowns that may have existed—even if in my subconscious. Nonetheless, I was still pleased that I felt no sensation of flames licking at my gluteals. Actually, I was again part of a soothing, intense field of light, though I did not feel the sense of expansion that I had when I was part of the astral plane. Thoughts drifted through my existence . . . It felt like I was again in a dream, but *only* a dream—nothing more, nothing less . . .

More time passed—who knows how long—and the thought drifted through my existence that perhaps I was in some sort of purgatory. This came after a series of visions that repeated themselves over and over and over, despite my futile attempts to shut them out.

At times, I was swimming in a huge vat of chili being attacked by gigantic hallucinogenic mushrooms. At other times, the base of my neck was being squeezed by a huge vise that slowly cut off the blood flow to the back of my brain. Topping that off was an astral guide who kept taking me out into space, pushing me away, and letting me drift off aimlessly into nothingness . . .

At the end of seven days, a piece of lumber awoke from its slumber. I came to in a hospital bed feeling like a six-foot two-by-four. Even my eyeballs felt stiff. Seven days of drifting in and out of near consciousness (as was later reported to me) is not a good prescription for muscle flexibility. Shortly after I opened my eyes and refocused them, a familiar face pushed through the door and into my room, and my eyes started drifting shut again.

Schmitty was carrying a large pepperoni pizza and a big handful of mail. He had looked right past me when he entered the room, and as he put the pizza and the mail on the corner table, he dropped something in the process. I reopened my eyes and saw him bend over and pick up a light blue envelope and drop it back on the pile of mail. He sat down and opened the pizza box and grabbed a slice.

"You gonna share, or what?" I said in a raspy voice.

"Doc!" he yelled and came over and gave me a big hug.

"Careful, man," I said. "I feel like I've been run over by a garbage truck."

"As much as your talking sometimes drives me crazy, damn, it's good to hear you say something! The neurologist told us you would likely come to eventually, but we really didn't have any idea when. Here, sip some of this glass of water."

"So, just exactly *when* is it right now?" I asked, slowly sipping from the glass.

"About a week after you decided to play action hero and ended up damn near dead at the edge of the Mississippi River."

At that point I started feeling my torso with my right hand.

"What are you doing?" asked Schmitty.

"Feeling for bullet holes."

"You can keep touching yourself, but you won't find any."

"What the hell happened?" I asked, as pieces of detail began to flood into my brain.

"You sure you want to talk about this now?"

"Yes, right now!" I demanded. I was tired, and my brain was foggy, but I needed answers.

"All I can tell you is what the guy who pulled you out of the river told us. This guy, who was out for a walk on the river trail, came around the bend and saw you sneaking on the grass toward another guy—incidentally wearing a *sling* on his left arm—who had just pulled out a gun as he approached a woman. This woman—incidentally a tall *brunette*—was walking just ahead of him. He sees you take off and launch yourself toward this guy, and the next thing he hears is what sounds like a muffled gunshot and watches the two of you roll down the embankment into the river. He takes off running, and by the time he gets there, the other guy, who had been floating on his back downriver, is barely visible.

He sees you lying unconscious at the bottom of the embankment with your head in the water. The woman, who was wearing some big set of headphones, apparently mustn't have heard a thing, because she kept walking down the trail and didn't respond to his calls for help. Realizing he didn't have much time, he made his way down the rocky embankment and pulled your head out of the water. Fortunately, you were breathing, so he pulled out his cell phone and called 911. As he hung up, he looked both ways, and the floater and the woman were both gone."

"Now, Doc," he continued, "I can make some guesses here, but—"

"You don't need to make any guesses!" I yelled as I tried to sit up, but fell back into bed—partially from exhaustion and partially from embarrassment. My body was weak, but my brain was going a mile a minute.

"I'm sorry, Schmitty," I whispered as I closed my eyes. "You didn't deserve that."

"It's okay, man. With the head bonk you took on those rocks, I'll cut you some slack. Besides, I'm just glad you're okay."

It was time to come clean with Schmitty about everything that had happened from the beginning, including what happened at Saint John's, what I knew about Asmail, and about my tire blowout. I did so, sparing no details.

As I finished, I put my left hand on my forehead, realized the hand was bandaged, and shook my head a bit. "I just don't know anymore, Schmitty. I'm so damn confused. Right now is probably not a good time to try to figure this out, since I apparently was unconscious for a week, but I know I'm going to have a hard time trying to separate *true* reality from what I know I want reality to be. Right now, I have no idea if my vortex experience really happened, or if I just created it, or if three bowls of chili or some vascular abnormality created it . . . I have no idea—for sure—who, or what, was going on under the Plymouth Avenue Bridge, but apparently as a result, some guy—maybe Asmail, maybe not—went floating down the river . . . Did they find him?"

"No they didn't, and they dragged the river for several days. They didn't find a gun, either. Your eyewitness, however, made it perfectly clear what appeared to be going down, and the police have already exonerated you, though they do want to get a statement when you're up to it. Now, about the chili . . ."

"We'll talk about that later," I said as my nurse excitedly entered the room.

"You're back among the living!" she proclaimed. "I saw your heart rate jump up on the monitor and came in to check on you. Didn't think I'd find you awake and talking!"

"If he's awake, trust me, he'll be talking," said Schmitty.

I spent another full week in the hospital vacillating between the exuberance of being alive and the despair of trying to reassemble reality after coming so close to what I was certain was Joy. My spirits were buoyed by the fact that Schmitty walked in one day with my old cell phone in hand. Apparently Diggie had discovered it in the toolbox of the cherry picker. If all else failed, at least we could try to make another stab at finding the vortex.

Much of the time I spent in the hospital involved enduring all of the things that people on the other side of the stethoscope know quite well. Fortunately, excellent physical therapy and quality nursing care triumphed over numerous interruptions of sleep and marginal hospital food. The nursing staff, knowing who I was, took full advantage. When they ambulated me down the hall or sent me off for testing, they made certain that my gown was "tied" in the back. My southern exposure is nothing to write home about, but they weren't doing it for anyone's edification but mine.

Gradually regaining strength, I began to look forward to my discharge back to the outside world. Fortunately, my numerous visitors did not press me for details as to what had transpired, but I suspected the word had spread and that they had heard enough to satisfy their curiosity. Besides, I fully expected to get grilled later when I went back to work and when I caught up with my fishing buddies.

My headaches finally improved off of the medication, the staples were removed from the gash in the back of my head, and I could ambulate without hanging onto an IV pole. A repeat CT scan showed no obvious sequelae of hard head hitting even harder rock.

Schmitty brought me my mail and updates from the outside world, and I didn't bring up the subject of chili again, but I fully intended to—when I was ready for the answer.

Despite being a voracious reader, especially enjoying the newspaper, I didn't feel much like reading anything at all until the day before I was due to be discharged. There was a brown paper bag almost full of mail sitting beside my chair. I dumped it out on the bed and was going to start going through it, but then looked at the sheer mass of it and decided that paying bills could wait a few more days. I began stuffing it back in the bag, and as I was putting the last handful in, a light blue envelope fell out onto the floor.

I picked it up, and as I was stuffing it in the bag, the return address in the upper left corner caught my attention:

Midwest Sound Studios
403 N. 1st Ave.
Minneapolis, MN 55401

Sitting back down in the chair, I opened the envelope and began reading.

Dear Mr. Mann:

I hope this correspondence finds you in good health.

(*How ironic*, I thought.) I read on:

You may or may not be aware of Midwest Sound Studios, but we are a recording group based here in Minneapolis.

(I was aware of them.)

We are aware that you are currently in process with a copyright dispute over the song "Our Love Story (Is Ours Alone)."

We are aware of this information because we are a subsidiary of Allied Sound Group.

Information has come to our attention that should finally put this matter to rest. Please visit us in person at our offices at your earliest convenience.

Sincerely,

Jacob R. Wittrock
President

Interesting, I thought. I had no idea what "putting this matter to rest" actually meant, but it appeared that at some point I was going to have to go to the office of one Jacob R. Wittrock in order to find out. The formality of the letter and its relative lack of information made me suspect that Allied was about to crawl into a monster truck full of lawyers and try to run me over. "Good luck with that," I muttered as I stuffed the letter into the bag.

The next day Schmitty picked me up to drive me home. The Stang had long since safely been parked at my house. We were almost there when we turned and looked at each other almost simultaneously and said, "Beer?"

I figured two weeks had been long enough, and what could a pint of suds hurt anyway? We rolled into T. J. Hooligans and ordered a pitcher and two plates full of tacos. The place was busy as usual, and for me, it was good to be back in my element.

"Life is good," I mumbled through a mouthful of seasoned beef.

"Damn straight," came the response. "Damn straight."

Epilogue

One week later, work had decided that I still wasn't quite ready to come back because of my concussion and my bruised left hand, even though I disagreed. I was insanely curious as to whether my enhanced diagnostic and musical skills were still present, or if they had somehow disappeared with my head injury. Not even being able to play the guitar, I puttered around the house, paid my bills, and cleaned up the place. I dropped my backpack into the closet. Months later I would discover a small broadcast camera in it and recall a dream about how it might have gotten there.

Finally, I gave in to another curiosity—the visit to Midwest Sound Studios. I called ahead and announced my impending arrival.

It felt great to be back on the road driving again. It was a beautiful day in June, as most days in June are here in Minnesota.

I headed up Highway 169 to 394 and into downtown. Only then did it strike me how close I would be coming to the place of my near demise. I decided I'd see how the meeting went and then decide if I wanted to drive back to the little park and walk down to the bridge. Guess I could sit there for a while and see if anyone familiar walked by . . .

I arrived at the location, fed the meter, and walked into a large stone building. Midwest's offices apparently took up half of the building, so they were much larger than I had assumed them to be. The directory told me that Mr. Wittrock's office was on the third floor, so I took the stairs.

Arriving, I was greeted by a male administrative assistant whose name tag read "Charles." "I'm here to see Mr. Wittrock," I said as I handed him the letter.

"Yes, we were expecting you. But you won't be seeing Mr. Wittrock today. We have scheduled a meeting with the vice president."

Before I could protest, Charles was halfway down a hallway to a door marked with the name J. Jarvie. He stood there until I arrived. "I have a meeting to attend," he said, "but you are expected, so go ahead and go in."

I stood outside the door and watched him go back down the hallway. I slowly opened the door and stood in its threshold. A large wooden desk dominated the room and was adorned with a computer, several CD cases, a pair of headphones, and a smartphone in a jeweled case. Across from me, and across the room, sunlight was streaming through windows covered by half-opened wooden blinds.

A figure was standing ahead of those windows and looking outside. I knew who she was long before she turned around . . .

About the Author:

Dr. Wayne Liebhard, a Minnesota native and family physician for twenty years, now practices in an emergency medicine clinic.

He has won numerous national awards as an author and songwriter, gaining special acclaim for his book *Elephants in the Exam Room—The Big Picture Solution to Today's Health Care "Crisis,"* and music from the album *Here—In Flyover Country.*

Besides his doctorate, he holds undergraduate degrees in the natural and social sciences from Saint John's University (MN), and his articles have appeared in numerous publications ranging from *Minnesota Physician* to *Mustang Monthly.*

He lives in Minnesota with his wife, Joy, dog, Oscar, and his Ford Mustangs. His classic rock band is still cranking out the tunes and releasing music videos.